Portrait of a Dog as a Young Artist

and

Other Short Stories

by

Eugene L. Mendonsa

This book is affectionately

dedicated to

Ann Templeton

Preface

As I have lived and worked in many different countries, these short stories reflect the life of a rolling stone. They are fiction, but are drawn from my experiences as an anthropologist who lived in Africa for nine years; my forty years in academia; my life in the art world; my love of animals; my political consciousness and people with whom I have come into contact throughout the years.

I have listed the thirty-two short stories in no particular order in the table of contents, but then, following this, I have categorized them by subject matter for your convenience, should you wish to, for instance, read a funny story or one about animals, etc.

Some of these stories are humorous, others are sad. Some are angry and some are light-hearted. That's the nature of life, isn't it? I hope you enjoy them.

About the Author

Dr. Eugene L. Mendonsa is an author, painter, filmmaker & a retired anthropologist. Known in the art community as "gino", Dr. Mendonsa is a graduate of Cambridge University in England. At present he paints and writes in New Mexico, where he is a contributing editor for *Southwest Living Magazine.* He is at work on a how to paint book with Ann Templeton and an academic book entitled: *The Fabrication of Domination.*

He has published numerous professional, business and fiction pieces, some of which have won awards. He also wrote and directed the documentary shown on PBS entitled: *Sisala Divination: The Mystic Tradition.* His books include: *The Politics of Divination*; *Continuity and Change in a West African Society: Globalization's Impact on the Sisala of Ghana; West Africa: An introduction to its history, civilization and contemporary situation;* and a murder mystery called: *Fishing for Clues.*

Some of his renowned photographs reside today in the Smithsonian Institution in Washington D.C. His graphic art has been used in college textbooks and magazines. His paintings hang in galleries, private collections and in institutions.

Table of Contents

Table of Contents by Category

1. *Portrait of a Dog as a Young Artist*

I am a world-renowned artist. I paint in oils, acrylic and pastel. I would paint in nearly any medium invented, as I dearly love the act of creating beauty on canvas, paper, wooden panels – on anything, really.

I have a very wonderful studio, which gets lots of light, thanks to the three big skylights and two walls made of floor-to-ceiling sliding glass doors. It is light and airy, being filled with lots of plants and a little waterfall that gurgles out delightful sounds. I usually have music playing in the background while I paint. It is a pleasant place to be. It is so wonderful that I often sit in the studio in my big rocking chair beneath one of the skylights and read when I am not painting.

I want to tell you about an event that happened the other day, which has to go down in the annals of animal oddities, if such a book exists. Anyway, I was luxuriating with a book by Dylan Thomas, entitled: *Portrait of an Artist as a Young Dog*, which surely he must have meant to be a pun on James Joyce's *Portrait of an Artist as a Young Man,* both being examples of *Künstlerroman* novels.

My mind was having difficulty concentrating on Dylan's work, which was a fine piece of writing; but I had a monster one-man show coming up and I needed to have many more paintings for it than I was producing at the moment. Furthermore, Art Loop was happening that weekend and I would no doubt sell some paintings as people sauntered through my studio looking for bargains. So my mind kept flitting back and forth between what I was reading, the need to produce more for the show and whether or not I should serve food for the Art Loop visitors.

About that time my cute little pug puppy waddled into the studio, jumped up in her favorite chair and dropped off into wherever dogs go when they sleep. I now had a further distraction as I tried to concentrate on *Portrait of an Artist as a Young Dog* because Cassie was apparently dreaming and yapping every so often.

I gave up and decided to paint something. I went to the closet where I keep my panels, selected a sixteen by sixteen and put it on the easel. The yip-yip and yap-yap was still bugging me, so I put some Cuban salsa music on the CD player and began to tone the canvas with a wash of transparent orange. The painting did not go well, though I got a lot of paint down, it just didn't gel as a work of art. In frustration I took it off the easel and set it aside, laying it flat on the small table to my left.

Just then the phone rang and I went into the house, which is attached to the studio, to answer it.

When I returned to the studio Cassie was nowhere to be seen. I was not worried because the door was open onto the garden and she always came and went as she pleased.

Then I noticed the little painted paw prints leading from my easel to the door. I walked over to the easel and saw that Cassie had jumped up on the side table and walked around in my wet painting. I normally paint in a fairly abstract fashion, but her meanderings in my painting had turned it into a non-representational painting to be sure.

I held the canvas up to the light and admired my dog's work. I kind of liked it. Then it occurred to me to play a joke on my customers who would be coming for Art Loop, many of whom were locals and friends of mine. I put the painting on the drying rack and forgot about it, going on to other things, including trying to finish *Portrait of an Artist as a Young Dog* and cleaning up Cassie's paws when she came in from the garden.

On the Friday before Art Loop, I framed Cassie's masterpiece and put it on the display wall along with my work, signing it in the lower right-hand corner: *Cassie*. Cassie had one and I had twenty-nine paintings to present to my unsuspecting public. I figured it would be a point of conversation to joke about the dog-produced canvas. *Thirty masterpieces*, I joked in my mind. *Well, twenty-nine anyway.*

When I opened my studio doors for Art Loop weekend, the customers were already waiting outside.

They filed in, some going straight for the cookies and coffee, others milling about looking at the paintings on the wall. To my great surprise, a patron came over and asked: "Who is this Cassie. I love her work."

"Uh...I...er..."

"How much is it?"

My joke was coming back on me. "Uh...let's see. It's a sixteen by sixteen. That's fifteen hundred dollars."

"I'll take it," said the patron. "It's lovely. I do so much like non-representational work."

Right then and there I vowed to put Cassie to work on a regular basis and that was the beginning of her career as a young, but not so aspiring artist.

Do art associations sponsor one-dog shows?

2. The Fish that Couldn't Talk

They had sent the American upcountry to one of South Africa's posh fishing resorts. It was a business trip, but he had a break between his work in Johannesburg and Cape Town, so they had paid for a couple of days at the spa, which was really a five star hotel sitting on a lake full of trout. The whole place revolved around fly-fishing, with a pricey fly shop, top-drawer restaurant, nice bungalows encircling the lake and several nearby trout streams and other lakes, each teaming with potentially hungry fish. There were separate bars for the men and women and lots of upper-end shops for the women to cruise while the men hunted down cruising fish. Women didn't fish there, the Yank noticed.

On his first morning there, the Yank had been surprised that there was frost on his patio table. This wasn't Kilimanjaro or Mt. Kenya! Then he remembered that even though he was in Africa, the resort stood at 8,000 feet, even though the terrain of the Transvaal was mildly undulating and relatively flat. South Africa had snow and ice at times, their winter being Europe's summer and so forth.

After a nice breakfast in the well-apportioned dining room, the staff had taken him out to a stream with two other fly-fishermen, one British chap and a South African fellow of British descent. Both were diehard dry fly enthusiasts, which meant they disdained using any fly that sank beneath the water to attract a trout.

The American, on the other hand, came equipped with a full range of flies: dry, wet and even bead-heads, which amounted to a wet fly tied with a tiny hollow brass ball attached to the head of the imitation. The ball acted as a flashy attractor, while at the same time sinking the fly quickly to where fish spend most of their time – on the bottom.

The two Brits, for that's the way the Yank saw them, were outfitted with the normal fly-fishing gear: vest, graphite rods, Hardy reels and double-taper lines. Neither had on waders, however, opting for Wellington boots, which they called "Wellies." The Yank had the same gear, but was using a weight-forward line and he wore lightweight chest-waders instead of the Wellies.

About nine-thirty that morning, the staff dropped them off at the gin-clear stream, which had been stocked with brown trout years ago by British colonials who had administered the Republic of South Africa before it became independent of Britain. The friendly black driver said he would return at noon with a box lunch and some white wine. The two Brits decided to fish upstream, while the Yank walked a mile or so downstream and then worked his way back up to the drop point.

It was about twelve-thirty when the Yank made it back. The driver had set up a table, replete with a linen tablecloth, three chairs and was laying out the luncheon vittles. Shortly afterwards, the two Brits came downstream and joined the Yank for lunch.

When fly-fishermen meet up like that the first thing they ask is: "How'd you do?" Stripping off his waders, that is what the Yank asked when he saw the two coming toward the table.

"Quite well, actually," replied the older, gray-haired man. "I caught one and my mate got two."

"How did you do?" asked the second fisherman, in a strong South African accent. The Yank hesitated, for he had caught over fifty fish in three hours, almost all on bead-headed wet flies. Judiciously he replied that he had caught only a "few."

On the second morning of the trip, the Yank was informed that a television crew would be arriving from Johannesburg to film a documentary on fly-fishing in South Africa. Rather than be ferried out to a stream or another lake, he chose to hang around the lodge and fish in the lake there and perhaps take a nice afternoon snooze in his nearby chalet. After all, there wasn't much sport in fishing the streams, as these trout had never seen a bead-headed wet fly and the Yank had been a fly-fishing guide in

Colorado in his younger days. As such, he knew that there was a lot more to fishing than catching fish.

That morning he worked the lake and caught quite a few fat browns, which he could see cruising the edges of the water, feeding mainly on rising nymphs, with an occasional "pig" rising to the surface to sip an emerging fly off the top. Catching them on wet flies proved far too easy, so the Yank switched to dry flies and took a few fish before going in for lunch.

When the television crew showed up and began to set up their cameras and equipment near the water's edge, the Yank wandered down to watch the filming. He noticed that the crew included a well-outfitted fly-fisherman, who looked like he was there for an Orvis catalog photo shoot. He certainly looked the part.

A longhaired chap, who seemed to be the director, got his equipment in place and then simply told his fly-fisherman: "Right then. Catch a fish." He made a hand gesture to his cameraman, who apparently started filming the green-clad fisherman.

The Yank watched as the young man beautifully cast a dry fly, looking like a stand-in for Brad Pitt in *A River Runs Through It*. He had the technique, dropping the fly softly on the water without hardly disturbing the surface. He did this again and again, but he didn't catch any fish.

The Yank noticed that the surface feeding that had been in some evidence while he was fishing earlier had now disappeared. The trout were no longer feeding on the top, but were still circling the shoreline taking an occasional bug below the surface. There were not many feeders left, but with his polarized sunglasses he could easily see an occasional German Brown swim by the camera crew.

The longhaired guy seemed to be getting upset with his fisherman, who continued to throw a marvelous line, graceful in every movement. He just wasn't catching fish. Not one. The Yank watched as the scene dragged on with no results.

"We've got to catch a fish!" the director shouted. "This is about how great fishing is in South Africa. We can't go back with no fish in the bloody thing!" The South African director was getting red in the face and his fisherman, with all the right gear, had egg on his.

The Yank sauntered down to where the director was frantically waving his arms, which of course was the opposite of what any right-minded fisherman would be doing near cruising fish in a gin-clear lake. "If I might be of some assistance," he offered. "I can catch one for you, if you would like."

The flushed director looked at the Yank as if he had leprosy, actually taking a step back. "You're a Yank, aren't you?"

"Yes. Yes I am and I'm a Yank that can catch you a fish for your film." They weren't getting off on the right foot, it seemed.

"I'm not sure that is the case. Nigel here is one of the best fishermen in the RSA. If he can't catch one today we will just have to come back for another shoot when the fish are biting."

"They are feeding right now," replied the Yank calmly. "I can get one on for your cameras anytime you wish." The gauntlet was thrown down.

"Hah!" snorted the director.

"Sure you can, mate," chimed in the well-outfitted guide.

Several of the crewmembers sniggered. The black driver who had been at lunch the previous day with the fishermen was standing nearby. He walked over and whispered something to the director, who looked over at the Yank. After a discussion with the South African guide, the director approached the Yank. He said, nodding his head in the direction of the black driver, "My friend says I should let you have a go."

"Sure," replied the Yank, "just give me a second and I'll get my rod."

After returning from his cabin with a nine-foot four-weight Scott rod, the American fisherman made two casts and hooked a six-pound brown trout that had been lazily circling the lake. As was his habit, the Yank yelled when he hooked the fish and talked to it. "There you go, baby!"

When he landed and released the fish, giving it a symbolic kiss, he said: "Okay sweetheart, back to the water with you."

The guide sulked off, standing stiffly near the crew's Land Rover.

The director was again waving his arms wildly. "No, no, no!" he shouted at the Yank.

"You wanted a fish for your footage. I got you a fish."

"But this is about South African fishing. You can't talk like that. The audience will know you're an American." The way he said *American* made it sound an awful lot like a swear word – the *A*-word.

And so the scene was shot over again, this time with a five-pound fatty taking a sinking bead-headed mayfly. With his severely bent rod raised to the sky, the trout was picturesquely fought and gently brought to the lowered net without a disparaging word uttered by the smiling Yank.

3. The Roswellians

Sarah Burns sat at her console, headset on, listening to the chatter of the astronauts. She had always been stuck at the desk through several space flights during her long career at NASA. In fact, she had never been out of Florida in her entire life and rarely left the community surrounding Cape Canaveral. She called herself a "space groupie."

The astronauts were gabbing with the four men and two women on the ISS, the International Space Station. Sarah thought it rather mundane prattle for people who held advanced degrees and were involved in exploring the frontiers of space. Most of the ISS personnel had been to the Moon at one time or another and the astronauts on the space ship were headed for Mars – where NASA planned to build a new scientific outpost, similar to the one now on the moon. Why then discuss which Rocky movie was the best? As a self-proclaimed "space junkie," Sarah always hoped for deeper, scientific discussions. She wanted *foix gras* and got potato chips. As usual, Sarah was bored.

Then it happened – that moment she had been waiting for in all her dull, spinstered life. It was *foix gras en plus*. "We've got a sighting!" There was excitement in Jim Rogers' voice, the Commander of the Mars Mission. "We see something, ISS. Notify Canaveral."

"They're plugged," came the terse reply from the space platform. Canaveral was on the wire.

Sarah hit the red button on her console: "Whatayagot, Jim?"

"Sarah? You still on duty."

"Got no life, Jim. You know that?"

"Hey, NASA's a great lover, don't ya know."

"You're a *mean* man, Jim Rogers. Tell me what you got up there."

"We're coming up on Mars – the planet not the candy bar."

"George Burns you're not. Tell me."

"The advance telescope picked up what appears to be a settlement."

"A what?" asked Sarah incredulously.

"Seems there is a town on Mars."

"A what?!" exclaimed two astronauts simultaneously from the ISS.

"Cameras don't lie."

In the background Sarah heard a shipmate ask her Commander: "Do you want a zoom?"

"I always wanted to be a peeping Tom. Zoom it Mary."

There were a few moments of silence, then: "Wow!"

"What?" asked Sarah, the muscles in her neck clinching. She would need an extra glass of Merlot in front of her fake fire tonight.

"Do you see that?" came an unidentified voice from the space ship.

"What?!!!" screamed Sarah into the mike. Her supervisor gave her the "cool it" signal from his adjacent console. "I mean, what have you got Commander?"

"He's pulling our leg," commented her supervisor sardonically, covering his microphone with a tobacco-stained hand. "I've told him more than once not to joke around. This is serious stuff. Senators and taxpayers are listening in."

Silence.

"What have you got Commander?" repeated Sarah.

"Mary, zoom in more. Can you zoom in more?"

"Yes sir," came the reply with a Texas twang.

Sarah strained to hear something – anything. She was more excited than when she saw that Elvis impersonator at Disney World.

"My golly!" exclaimed Commander Rogers. That's a giant 1947 in rocks or something."

"What are you seeing Jim?" It was the stern voice of the mission supervisor sitting next to Sarah. "You wanna let us in on it?"

"I dunno, Jack. Maybe my eyes are playing tricks on me."

"No sir," said the Texas voice. "It spells out 1947 right in the center of what appears to be houses. Some sort of community. Mars is …" The Texas voice cut out. Crackle-crackle-crackle.

"Inhabited," said Sarah softly.

Jack Peters spoke firmly: "Jim. We can't joke about this on the air. People are listening. We even got press guys here."

"Well, they're gonna have one hellava story then. This camera's picking up what seems a town built around some kind of plaza with the numerals 1947 in the center of the square. We're headed right for it."

"This is crazy," someone on the ISS said.

"I got movement, sir." It was the voice of the Texas gal.

"Yeah, I see it too."

"See what?" exclaimed Sarah, her voice strained. The speaker on her console began to crackle. She was losing transmission. "What are you seeing Jim?"

Crackle-crackle-crackle. "Well, it looks like…" crackle-crackle "a…" crackle-crackle "group of…" crackle-

crackle. Silence.

"They're in the dead zone," said Jack Peters, the mission supervisor in Canaveral. "We won't have 'em again until the Fiji station picks 'em up."

* * * * * *

The next three days of Sarah's life were a dream. This was what she had waited for all those years at her desk in Cape Canaveral. This was a scientific breakthrough. This was world news. There were beings on Mars. People. Well, not people like us, but they could communicate. Some even spoke English, although with a very strange accent. One of their spokespersons sounded vaguely like Edward R. Murrow, like he was delivering the evening news every time he spoke. If he was a he. Sarah wasn't sure of the gender thing yet.

Sarah took a sip of her coffee. It was cold. So was her apartment. She pulled her robe tighter. It wasn't supposed to be cold in Florida, she thought.

"And there aren't supposed to be little green men on Mars," she muttered aloud. Tango, her cat, said: "meow" and curled up in her lap.

Sarah stared at the newspaper on her kitchen table. She hadn't even been born in 1947. She would have to read up on it. No doubt there were news reports and stuff. Vaguely she remembered seeing some kind of UFO television program once. On the *Discovery Channel* or something.

Still, the headline was startling. And thrilling.

Absently, Sarah pushed her cat off her lap, got up and refilled her morning coffee. When she sat down again, the newspaper headline was still there. It hadn't changed and she hadn't dreamed it up.

ROSWELLIANS ON MARS!

Sarah didn't even know where Roswell was. Somewhere in the west. Somewhere dry she knew. Desert country.

This wasn't some sensational rag at the checkout line at Wal-Mart. It was *The Miami Herald.*

Sarah hit the button on the clicker and the TV jumped to life. Tango leaped onto the kitchen table to watch, though he didn't know or care about the news.

Sarah brought the sound up and heard the broadcaster saying: "… and this story just gets more amazing all the time." He turned his head toward the tight-faced blond on his left, as if he expected her to make some profound statement at this point.

All she could muster was: "It certainly does, Ralph."

The third person at the news desk, apparently the

weatherman, added: "I guess we're going to have to start doing the weather report for the Red Planet now," and the three broadcasters all tittered like school kids at an off-color joke.

"Who would have suspected that the whole Roswell thing was true?" asked the square-jawed anchorman.

"Who, indeed?" chimed the anchorwoman, stupidly.

"I guess that's why the Martians named their town Roswell and called themselves the Roswellians," put in the weatherman.

"And wasn't it 1947 when that event happened in New Mexico?" asked the blond, as if *she* was from another planet.

Sonorously, the anchorman said: "It certainly was, Marsha. But our research department tells me that back then people in the USA just thought that it was a hoax, that the debris was simply from a broken weather balloon."

"Or an Air Force experiment or something," put in the weatherman.

The blond flashed perfect teeth and declared: "I think its cute that these Roswellians, as they call themselves … that they made that big 1947 monument in their town."

"Right, Marsha. It is a new kind of *human* interest story, isn't it?"

They all chortled again, as if they were laughing alone on some lost island beach.

"And didn't the astronauts who visited the Martian town say that the townsfolk, if we can call them that, had put up human faces all over there town?" asked the weatherman, rhetorically.

The TV screen blinked and showed large posters of human beings on the streets of the Martian town. The camera then panned to large human-shaped balloons swaying in the Martian breeze. They had some strange writing on them.

When the footage was over, the three anchorpersons resumed their chatter. The stiff-haired blond was talking: "You know Ralph, you should go up there and interview the director of that museum."

"Yes I should, Marsha. The astronauts said it was filled with all kinds of plastic human dolls, newspapers from the forties and fifties – really all kinds of interesting memorabilia they'd picked up in New Mexico."

There was a pause in their banter and the three broadcasters looked at each other nervously, as if they didn't know how to get out of the story. Then the blond thought she had an exit line to fuel the laughs: "Well Ralph, you really should take that assignment on Mars. Think of all the frequent flyer miles you'd rack up."

Sarah hit the off button before she was subjected to the guffaws.

****

After weeks of news stories about Mars, Sarah Burns was tired of little green men, which is what the rag sheets at the checkout stands were calling the Roswellians, although they weren't green. Their skin was kind of a silvery color, with a real sheen to it, almost like the material on a fine evening gown. And some were little, but some were big – in fact, they spanned the same height range of, say, people in the Third World on Earth. Short, but in wide-ranging heights.

Sarah was in another boring period at work. There were no space flights at the moment and she only had the ISS people to talk to, those semi-permanent residents on the International Space Station; but they were like family by now. And who wants to talk to your family all the time?

Sarah was glad to be home after a tedious day of clock-watching. She flicked on the TV, despite the fact that she knew she would have to watch Ralph, Marsha and the weatherman, whose name Sarah could never remember; and, as had been the case since the Roswellians were discovered on Mars, they would be talking about every dreary detail they had pried out of the astronauts when they returned from the now famous Mars Mission. One newspaper ran the headline: *1947 in 2087*. Of course, that was a reference to the alleged sighting and crash of UFOs near Roswell, New Mexico in 1947. The astronauts had left Cape Canaveral in 2086, but safely returned in the following year – 2087.

Sarah had to endure an insipid commercial about the new Intel chip that functioned as well as any laptop in the early years of the 21st Century; and, being an entire computer on a microchip, for $1,295, it could be implanted in your skull and connected, through wavelengths, to your brain. Intel guaranteed that it would outlast your brain. Intel = one; human brain = nil.

After the next commercial with the nauseating pink bunny and his drum, the handsome and beautiful anchors came on and droned on about the latest conflict in the Middle East, a terrorist threat stymied near Ground Zero in NYC and so on. Violence and more violence.

Then the bombshell. "So Ralph, I hear you have an exciting assignment that will take you away from us for a while." It was the sugar sweet voice of the impeccably blond anchorwoman.

"It is true, Marsha and I am excited about being out where the action is again."

Following the lines on the teleprompter, Marsha asked: "And tell us Ralph, where will you be on assignment?"

Ralph flashed capped teeth that would have made any dentist happy: "I've been assigned to accompany the next Mars Mission. We blast off next month. I'm going to be the first newsman to interview the Roswellians."

"Well isn't that a feather in your cap. Of course, we will all miss …"

Sarah clicked off the set. She didn't like to feel such intense envy, but after all, she had put in years of service behind her meticulous desk at the Cape and she would never set foot on Mars or any other planet. It did not occur to her that she wanted to go into space and yet, ironically, she had never been out of Florida right here on earth.

****

Ralph Marshall had taken the pill the Commander gave him, which would allow him to breath normally in the thin atmosphere of Mars. He was glad astronauts no longer had to wear those bulky suits, but could simply coat their bodies with a special compound developed by Monsanto, which provided protection against harmful rays from the sun.

Ralph checked to see that his cameraman was ready to go and off they went. It was to be a great interview. Ralph was proud of the fact that he had persuaded one of the Roswellian city officials to allow him to film their home life, to actually get inside one of the odd conical-shaped houses in Roswell, Mars. Ralph smelled Pulitzer.

After filming Mrs. Martian in her kitchen, Mr. Martian in his den, Ralph asked to see the kids' rooms. Mr. Martian proudly led them down the hall to a room that was decorated not unlike that of the average teenager in the USA. It had wall-posters, a bed that appeared to have been hastily made and the floor was littered with all sorts of teen stuff. In the center sat a small, silver kid with his bug-eyes focused on a large black X-Box. He didn't seem to be very interested in the tall visitor from Earth or the guy behind him with the bulky camera and a bright light.

Ralph thrust a microphone in the kid's face and asked: "So, sonny. What are you playing on the X-Box?"

The Martian kid looked at the anchorman as if he was from another planet and sourly replied: "War games."

"War Games?" Ralph acted surprised. "Just like my kids at home." Chuckle – chuckle. The cameraman cackled too, for better effect on the tape.

"And what is the name of the war game, sonny?"

"Uh, perhaps we should leave the boy to his pastime," the dad quickly said. He put his spindly fingers on Ralph's arm.

Professional that he was, Ralph pressed ahead: "Tell all our viewers on Earth, what is the name of your video game, son?

The boy threw a nippy glance at his dad, who shrugged his bony shoulders and turned his palms to the red Martian sky, tilting his slightly enlarged head to the side as he did so. At the same time, thin eyebrows went up above enormous eyes.

With the go ahead from his father, the boy rose to his feet and proudly announced: *Invasion of Earth.* Ralph looked down at the frozen screen on the video machine. It said: "Earthlings Die!"

"Pan in on that," he told his cameraman. "We've got a human…a *Martian* interest story here."

****

Sarah lit her fake fire and settled back to watch the C-Span re-run of Ralph Marshall's appearance before the Senate Armed Services Committee. His career was really taking off. His interviews on Mars would surely garner him all kinds of awards and a chance at an anchor spot at CNN. And here he was on C-Span entering the Senate Office Building to be questioned about his findings on Mars.

Sarah thought the anchorman looked confident. He shook a few hands of well-known reporters in the audience and then took his seat behind an enormous table. He was facing a gaggle of Senators.

The Chairman banged his gavel on an oval piece of

oak and began: "Mr. Marshall, you have already taken the oath. We need to know if you found any evidence that the Roswellians, as they call themselves, are hostile to the United States.

"Mr. Chairman, the Roswellians are as normal as any family in Sinclair Lewis's *Main Street* or on *Leave it to Beaver*."

"Are you saying they are not only not a threat, but boring too?" asked the Chairman, playing to the crowd. His tedious joke got polite snickers throughout the Senate chamber.

"I'm saying that they appear to be normal family people.

"Well then, what about this anti-American video game you found in the X-Box?"

"Senator, it wasn't anti-American. If anything, it was anti-Earthling."

"Same thing," snorted the conservative Republican Senator from Iowa.

Ralph continued: "But it wasn't even that. It was just a harmless kid game. We have much worse videos here on Earth."

"But that's normal 'kill the bad guys' stuff. These are aliens. Are we in any danger from these Martians?

Having interviewed several of them, what is your opinion?"

Ralph hesitated. Sarah thought he was playing to the cameras now. He raised his right hand for emphasis: "Mr. Chairman, I think we are in much more danger from videos right here on Earth than from anything the Roswellians are doing."

****

Sarah was at her desk at Cape Canaveral when her boss rushed in with a newspaper. He waved it about, as if he was swatting mosquitoes.

"What's up Jack? We got problems?" They had been worried lately about how the hearings on Mars would affect NASA's funding.

"Just the opposite. Just the opposite, Sarah!" He threw the newspaper down on her desk.

Sarah stared at the headline. It read:

SENATE VOTES TO SEARCH MARS FOR WMD

Sarah looked at her boss. He had a broad smile on his pink face. She thought he looked like Porky Pig. The veins in his fat neck were bulging like Arnold Schwartzenegger's muscles.

"Do you realize what this means for our program?" Jack Peters almost shouted, snatching up the newspaper. "We are going to Mars again to search for Weapons of

Mass Destruction. President Cush just went on television and announced that we are preparing preliminary plans for a preventative war against the Roswellians. Just in case, but WMD, Sarah. That's our funding ticket for the next few years!"

"Another search for WMD? Preventive war?" asked Sarah incredulously. "Didn't we do that once?"

****

Sarah, who had been transferred to the Spaceport in New Mexico, read the *Albuquerque Tribune* with her morning coffee. The headline read:

U.S. TROOPS INVADE MARS!

The front-page article indicated that the Generals planned to take Roswell, Mars first and then deal with any other brand of Martians they may encounter. As she read further through the paper, she came upon a related story about how the invasion was, in part, justified by the Roswellians' invasion of Earth at Roswell, New Mexico in 1947. On the same page was an advertisement by a well-known producer of video games for an X-Box version of: Invasion of Mars.

Sarah stroked her cat, which didn't seem to know or care about invasions, real or imaginary. This was Sarah's first day off in days, what with the troops funneling through the Spaceport on their way to conquer tiny silver people calling themselves the Roswellians. Sarah had little to do with them, having been assigned to get a special rocket ship ready for the newly expanded WMD search team. They had first priority in the launch sequence because President Cush personally authorized giving them preference, presumably to find weapons of mass destruction to justify the Mars attack.

The cat got tired of being petted and jumped off the kitchen table and headed for her bowl of Friskies. Sarah wondered if only the human strain of life waged war. Certainly she had seen enough animal violence in TV documentaries about the Serengeti in Africa or monkeys in the Amazon, but premeditated, organized – even "preventative" – assaults on less powerful people seemed to her "first-cup-of-coffee-brain" to be a very human endeavor. Sarah knew she would have to fight the urge to give in to cynicism and sadness today, maybe for longer than that. *Anyway, I have my cat.*

****

It had been months and Linda Vasco was fed up. She headed for the billet of the head of the WMD Search Unit, Larry Spacek. She found him looking over maps of the Martian interior, the lands beyond the Martian town of Roswell.

"Larry, we gotta talk."

Larry looked up and Linda could see the resignation

in his face.

"Yeah, I know."

"Are you ready to write the report?" Linda was referring to the report to the President on their failure to find any WMDs on Mars.

Larry shoved back from the map table. His shoulders slumped. "Yeah, yeah. We gotta do it, I guess."

"This war has been a farce, Larry. We have to face up to it and we have to tell the American people they were misled."

"Yeah, I was thinking about being misled. *We* were misled. Seems governments are good at that."

Linda had never heard her boss talk like this. "Well, that might be a little strong."

"I don't think so, not if you do a little research, read a bit. Before we came to Mars I had just finished a book by Daniel Ellsberg called *Secrets*. It lays out clearly how the U.S. government lied to the American people about Vietnam. And we all now know how we were lied to about the Iraq invasion back in the early years of this century. Now this stupid assault on these innocent people on Mars."

"Wow," exclaimed Linda taking a chair across from to Larry. "Stupid! You gonna use that in the report?"

There was a long pause and Linda wondered if her

boss had heard her, then he said in a small, but resigned, voice: "Maybe. Maybe it's time."

****

Lieutenant Matthews knocked on the General's door.

"Come!"

Matthews entered, saluted and stood at attention.

"At ease. Sit. Speak." The General was a man of few words.

The Lieutenant tried to follow suit. "Not good."

"What we thought?"

"Yes sir. We've stirred up a hornets nest."

"Foreign insurgents?

"Yes sir. Here's a list, although we can't identify all of them. Some are from Pluto, others from Venus. Some we don't know."

"So we're not just killing Martians?"

"No sir. Seems other Planetarians have come to fight in support of their brothers."

"Planetarians?"

"We don't know what else to call them. They all look different. Our interrogators tell me that they have different languages and cultures, but somehow our attack on the Martians created a backlash and brought them together."

The General hung his head. He had heard it all before. He hated killing. He hated war. He had not even wanted to go to West Point, but his father was a General in the Iraq war. Footsteps of his father and all that. *He told me. I've heard all this before. And we're gonna lose this one too.*

****

Sarah picked Tango up from the cat doctor, where she got her yearly checkup. She was fine, even if the world wasn't. *They really botched it. Now we've ticked off every civilization on every planet within reach. Blowback!*

Sarah had just finished reading an old book, which told an old story. But, unfortunately, there seems no end to the story. It goes on. The book was: *Blowback: The Costs and Consequences of American Empire* by Chalmers Johnson. It was published way back in the year 2000.

Sarah was shaking her head as she drove through the streets of Las Cruces. It occurred to her that the name of this New Mexico town had an ironic connection to the fiasco on Mars. *Las Cruces means The Crosses. The attack on Mars was based at the Spaceport near here. One more cross to bear. Crosses blowing back.*

Tango sat in the passenger's seat watching his

mistress. He wondered why she seemed perplexed. Tango wanted her to be happy. Happy as a cat.

****

The final report on the Mars fiasco came out in 2151, a year after the Americans admitted defeat and signed a peace treaty with the Planetarians, as they were now called, all those beings in outer space that had rallied in support of the Martians.

The report, compiled by a Blue Blood Commission appointed by the Congress, stated that the war on Mars was not only misguided, based on fallacious fears about WMDs, but also very costly in human life (discounting the loss of non-human life, Martians, Plutonians, Venetians, etc. – though no good records were kept on *their* casualties since they were not humans). It noted the following comparative figures: In World War II over 400,000 soldiers died; in Vietnam over 58,000; Iraq (including the Desert Storm) saw over one million U.S. and coalition soldiers die (no one kept track of insurgents or collateral deaths of civilians). By comparison the Mars Fiasco, as it was now popularly called in the press, killed over three million U.S. troops over its fifty-year duration. This was attributed to the superior weapons some of the insurgent Planetarians brought to Mars and the guerilla warfare tactics that were so hard to combat.

The report questioned not only why the President

started the war, but why he let it go on so long and why subsequent men who sat behind the oval desk did little to stop it. Even that female President didn't do anything. And why did they follow Cush's lead year after year and up troop levels sent into space?

The report was widely heralded in America and abroad. It seemed that, finally, human beings were getting tired of war. It wasn't only the liberal press and radio shows like *Democracy Now* that praised the Commission's findings, but also reporters on *Fox News* and conservative talk show hosts.

While the world was going gaga over the newfound idea that, perhaps, we should give peace a chance, one story got very little play in the media. The mayor of Roswell, NM laid a wreath at what was assumed to be the famous crash site at William "Mack" Brazel's farm, which the city fathers had purchased and constructed as a disc-shaped monument.

Standing before the monument the mayor said: "The people of New Mexico, and especially those of us lucky enough to live in Roswell, are assembled here today to honor the war dead in the Mars Fiasco, but not just the human beings who died in that ill-advised war; but also the Planetarian dead. Today, on this historic occasion, we in Roswell and all throughout New Mexico affirm that life is precious wherever it is found. Let the peace commence and endure."

The speech by the mayor brought hearty applause and it was followed by the Governor of New Mexico, who said similar things and got an equally rousing round of applause.

****

While all this was going on in Roswell, in a graveyard in Las Cruces, a cat slipped through a hole in the chain link fence and made its way to a grave, the headstone of which read: *Here lies one of ours: Sarah Burns (2033-2099) – NASA*. Ever since her death a series of cats, all resembling her beloved Tango, made a pilgrimage to the gravesite. They didn't make speeches or lay any wreaths on her grave. In fact, they merely sat there and preened themselves and then they left. But they came continuously throughout the years, one after another, each of a slightly different stripe, but all with a certain familiar look about them.

They were still coming when the people of Roswell had forgotten that there was a war monument in the farm once owned by William "Mack" Brazel.

4. *The United States of Hummerica*

The year was AD 3208, a Presidential election year in Hummerica, which the United States had been renamed when the Hummer Corporation took over the government. The President was no longer elected by the people, or from *all* the people; but he was inaugurated after an election within the Board of Directors in the company. And *he* would always be a he, as the Board did not allow women members. All congressmen, and a couple of token congresswomen, came from upper management in the corporation, with a handful coming from General Motors, the parent corporation of the Hummer line of automobiles.

Of course, some progressives at Berkeley and Boulder had objected to a corporation taking over what had passed for a democracy, but since the majority of people in the old United States were too busy buying things and hanging out at the mall to care about politics, the transition had gone pretty smoothly.

Intellectuals took to calling the new era "Ho-Hummerica." Anyway, voting had fallen to record lows just prior to the Hummer Corporation taking power anyway. The switch away from democracy kind of crept up on "the people" and no one really listened to the scatterbrains at *Democracy Now* or *Reclaim Democracy*; or even to the moderates at *Common Cause*. They got what was mistakenly called "news" from the *Fox Channel*. Propaganda has many synonyms.

Some had thought it possible that Toyota Motors might grow big and powerful enough to take over the feeble government in Washington DC, but the Hummer Corporation had scored great strides in wealth and power with their innovative move, placing a fifty-caliber machine gun atop their AD 3200 models. This stroke of genius put them far ahead of any other companies in the United States, even surpassing the former number one, the corporation named Marijuana Inc., which was a government-run company whose job it was to keep the people happy and buying things.

Of course, the Hummer Corporation took over Marijuana Inc. and improved distribution of its product, which was now grown in many Midwest farms as a staple and profitable crop. The USA had even been able to balance its budget; finally, thanks to getting their hands on all the Marijuana tax money they had been losing for decades. Now the Hummer Corporation had their fat, greedy hands on this windfall.

Besides an increase in tax revenue from the formerly banned substance, research at the National Science Foundation had shown that stoned Hummericans bought twice as much crap as sober ones. Drunks were somewhere in the middle. In any case, another Einstein at the Hummer Corporation went on to create a special Hummer, which was, effectively, a giant bong, with engine heat feeding through tubes laden with periodic injections of pot and with the fumes going to each passenger seat. It was kind of a new fuel injection system. The driver had no tube, for obvious reasons, but it was common knowledge that he could get moderately high by simply breathing exhaled fumes within the airtight Hummer. National Safety Administration tests showed that such a driver had only zero point two more accidents than a sober one. The Hummer Corporation quickly banned Mothers Against Drunk Driving (MADD), Alcoholics Anonymous (AA) and Narcotics Anonymous (NA). Driving under only zero point two influence was now okay.

The machine gun was a real marketing coup. The armed vehicles sold like hotcakes. The CHVV (Combo Hummer – machine gun atop the bong with wheels) sold better than hotcakes. They were more popular than pussy in a Naval port.

The armed Hummer was advertised as the solution to the road rage problem. Although the cannon on top was designed to fire only rubber bullets, Americans loved the idea that, if ticked off by someone on the road, they could simply hit a button on the dash and the gun's computer would quickly survey the videotape of the thirty seconds prior to the button being pressed. With a laser pointer, the enraged driver then could find the culprit on tape; click on him and then the gun would swivel and lock onto the culprit. Then the offender's car would be sprayed with a volley of rubber bullets, denting the car and sometimes breaking a window or two. (It was common knowledge that street gangs had figured out how to substitute real bullets for the ersatz ones).

Only about two thousand deaths a year were reported in connection with the Hummer Corporation's innovation, which the Board of Directors deemed an acceptable level of violence, given the profits from the *Harm*-vee, as it was dubbed by the progressive press. *Fox News* called it a "darling little vehicle." Some progressives thought it was neither small nor adorable.

Of course, there was a much higher death rate among the gangs that were using live ammo, but this was seen as a social good and no one lost any sleep over it, though some progressive rag sheets made a fuss about collateral deaths, such as when a gang-owned Hummer sprayed bullets at another Hummer full of rival gang members and killed everybody on the street at the same time. *Pacifica Radio* went wild, however, wanting to stay in business, the *New York Times, The Washington Post, CNN* and all mainstream media kept quiet about the matter. *Fox News* hinted that the dead might have been gang members themselves, or at least related to some.

Before installing the machine guns on their vehicles, the Hummer Corporation bought up the company that produced rubber bullets and re-fitted their machines to manufacture special bullets that would only work in the Hummer guns. Thus, the guns would not fire any bullets not produced by the Hummer Corporation's subsidiary. The bullet division's production went from six million bullets to forty billion a year. To counter any claims that Hummer was engaging in monopoly capitalism, they launched a public relations campaign that stressed the fact that the US of H was deeply committed to the principles of free trade.

Special amusement parks opened where people could roam around and practice shooting at dummy automobiles. A video game hit the market shortly thereafter that allowed people to hone their skills with a virtual machine gun mounted on a virtual Hummer. Kids and adult drones were virtually ecstatic.

There was some political backlash from the Humane Society when rubber bullets killed a Pit Bull in the back of a pickup outside of Midland, Texas; but the storm passed and the profits of the Hummer Corporation continued to rise, as did their political clout in Washington DC. The press paid little attention to the fact that an elderly woman returning from the grocery store was killed in the same flurry of bullets that hit the cute, little square-faced puppy.

Given America's central value – individualism – the Law mandating that every Hummerican had to own a Hummer did not go down well at first. Before the *coup d'état*, Americans had always liked their ability to buy any kind of car they wanted, even shoddy American ones or tight-as-ticks Asian ones. Nevertheless, the law was pushed through the ersatz congress, as some called it; a law that required each and every Hummerican to buy a Hummer and no other models could be driven. However, in five years time, even those autos had to be replaced by a magnificent Hummer. The new government placed a three hundred percent tax on bicycles and any other means of moving about that didn't involve a Hummer. Walking and jogging were discouraged. Marathons were banned as being bad for one's health. Statistics were publicized that between four and six marathoners died each year while running. It didn't matter that this was much lower than deaths due to rubber bullets.

Hummer banned the Hell's Angels and Hogs were not allowed on public roads. The company did open a new division, however, that produced a Hummer Hog, which was a small Hummer-looking motorcycle, plus they began to market a whole new line of black leather clothing to go with the new bike. In gratitude, bikers annually held noisy parades in Hummerica's major cities celebrating the sixth of June, which was the new Independence Day; being the date Hummer took over the government.

This governmental order had a compliance rate of sixty-nine point six percent, as there were tax incentives for owning a Hummer and other perks too numerous to mention. The other thirty-one point four percent of Hummericans were given five years to comply or they were to be shipped back to their country of origin. This was called the STB (Send Them Back) plan, again devised by the Board of Directors at Hummer. Furthermore, the Board felt that it would mainly affect people who didn't look or talk like Board members or their family and cohorts. Another social good.

If no country of origin could be determined, these deviants were to be sent to Liberia, which was a country in Africa originally established as a place where the US government could dump slaves captured at sea. As the corporation had a fund set aside to assist any Hummerican who wished to voluntarily return to their ancestral homelands, emigration rates rose dramatically after the introduction of the STB program.

There were brief demonstrations in front of the White House but the Hummer Corporation bought off the leaders by giving them and everyone in their families a brand new Hummer in the color of their choice. Reluctant leaders were given Hummers and cash. Some of the more stubborn dissidents entered the STB program involuntarily.

After that, Ford, Chrysler and all the Japanese and German car companies were closed, not by any governmental mandate, but simply by economics. Nobody was buying their cars and their production lines ground to a halt. Only car buffs were allowed to buy what was left in the showrooms, although they could only drive them on private property, not on public roads. It really was true: what was good for General Motors was good for Hummerica.

And there was some grumbling in élite circles and in the Op Ed pieces in the *New York Times, Washington Post* and the *Christian Science Monitor*. This mini-storm of dissent emerged when the Hummer Corporation passed a law allowing any illegal immigrant full citizenship if he or she bought a Hummer. At first, this did not take hold. People struggling to make a living working three minimum wage jobs had little left over to buy an expensive car like a Hummer. Or any time to drive one. Then the Hummer Corporation provided them with zero financing on one hundred year loans and car dealerships along the Mexican border sold out overnight and back orders went into months.

The members of the Hummer Corporation's Board of Directors drew up another plan to give pardons to any federal prisoners who purchased a Hummer; but it was eventually shelved because the company's actuaries determined that the cost to the corporation of fighting the crime wave this would unleash on the streets of United States of Hummerica (USH) would far supercede the profits generated by the program, which was called by Board members the "cars not bars" plan. In the end they voted for "bars over cars."

Some of the advertising guys in the firm employed by the Hummer Corporation to promote the Hummer came up with a brilliant idea. They sponsored a contest in which artists could win Hummers and big cash by painting pictures of Hummers. The winners then had their artwork featured in ads and eventually it hung in the corporate headquarters in Washington DC. What the corporate guys didn't understand at the time was that this ad campaign went on to spur the development of a whole new genre of art. The flurry of work revolving around the Hummer spawned the Hummerisionists, pushing the Modernists off the scene in New York galleries. If Andy Warhol had been alive, he would have painted a Hummer instead of a Campbell's soup can.

Most of the art was representational, some of it leaning toward abstraction. Some artists painted the vehicle in recognizable genres such as Impressionism, Abstract Expressionism or Cubism. One artist went too far when he sent in a blob of red paint in the middle of a huge white canvas. He titled his piece "Melting Hummer." The corporate types didn't like the implications of this, though they were hard pressed to say exactly why. His entry was rejected. However, the artist was nothing, if not persistent. For the next round of contest entries he re-submitted the same piece and re-named it "The Birth of the Hummer." It won first place and now hangs in the entryway of the company offices, located in what used to be called the White House.

As further marketing measures, the new corporate lawmakers in Washington quickly passed laws requiring every iPod and MP3 player to have built into it a laudatory salute to the Hummer Corporation. It played for thirty seconds after every one hundred songs. It was so well engineered, even the geeks at Microsoft and Apple couldn't figure out how to disable it. And the Hummer Corporation was all over television. It had at least ten infomercial channels on cable and satellite TV. The same was true for all video games. Before the kids could begin to numb their minds with the game itself; they had to endure thirty seconds of another kind of tranquilizer – the Hummer Corporation telling them how great they were, the Hummers that is; not the kids. The propaganda did, however, tell the kids how to become great: own a Hummer.

Hollywood got on the bandwagon, as usual, though from its new location in Las Vegas (due to the fact that global warming had drowned Los Angeles). The funny little movie about an animate auto, *Chitty Chitty Bang Bang,* was re-made with a cute little Hummer. The drag racing movie, *Rebel Without a Cause*, which made James Dean so famous, was re-shot with the bad boys in black leather jackets driving Hummers. In the scene where one idiot gets caught in his vehicle and goes over the cliff, film editors made changes. In the modern version, they had two cars fall to the canyon floor – a Hummer and an old Studebaker, which had been especially reconstructed for the movie. After they were shown hurtling over the edge, the camera panned to the canyon floor below. Of course, the Studebaker was a grease spot and the Hummer was unmarked. Andre Agassi was right: Image is everything.

At the Academy Awards, movie stars arrived in stretch Hummers, not the traditional sleek limos. No film, except an occasional one by a rogue filmmaker, ever won an Oscar without at least one Hummer in the picture, preferably in a car chase and always out-lasting the inferior cars driven by the bad guys.

All police forces across the United States of Hummerica were equipped with specially fitted Hummers. The cop versions had machine guns that used real fifty-caliber ammo. They regularly disappeared from police parking lots.

Madison Avenue did its part. Tall blonde women were photographed leaning seductively on Hummers. Brunettes with pumped up boobs and lips indicated, all too clearly, that if the boys bought a Hummer, she was included in the package. Sex and Hummer became synonymous. And sex *in* a Hummer was touted as being a lot easier than a forty-nine Ford or a thirty-seven Chevy.

That brings up demographics. The Hummer Corporation closed the offices of all do-gooder groups bent on sponsoring birth control. *The Population Bomb* was taken off the shelves of every library in Hummerica and banned on Amazon.com and Borders. All books by Paul Ehrlich were burned and banned. It was thought that more kids meant more sales, though advertisers were quick to tie larger families to the virtues of motherhood and other traditional values, playing down the bottom line aspect. Hummer executives devised a "This is Our Hummerica" advertising campaign with sentimental songs, pictures of pristine streams and the snow-capped mountains, cute little kittens, mothers hugging their children and all sorts of visualizations to link everything good to their big, ugly, gas guzzling vehicles. Lies can sometimes be comforting.

Even though the oil deep in the earth had long ago been exhausted, the gas guzzling aspect of the Hummer was not seen as much of a problem because it had been discovered that Mars and a couple of other nearby planets were full of oil and the Hummer Corporation had been fortunate early on to get the contract to design and build the pumps that sucked out the crude and sent it to large tanker spaceships through a spider web of pipelines to bring back to earth.

When one of these oil-packed shuttles collided with another, scientists had a new black hole in space on which to focus their telescopes. Again, it was only longhaired types at Berkeley or Boulder who brought up the thorny issue of the fact that space was now getting filled up with tiny (and some not so tiny) globules of oil whizzing around out there like minuscule black meteors. Astronauts complained that they couldn't keep the windshields of their shuttles clean, though the greater problem was that the presence of all the black globules was beginning to block out the sun, preventing its rays from reaching earth. This was, in fact, reversing global warming and archaeologists were eager to see the oceans drop again so they could move in and excavate places like San Francisco and Los Angeles. The CBS program *60 Minutes* did a piece on whether that Hollywood Sign would still be there.

It was shortly thereafter that *the* disaster happened. A major pipeline from the oil producing area on Mars to the landing site for the shuttles burst. The rupture was so large that repair crews could not stop the flow, the force of which ripped more and more of the line apart as precious hours slipped by. Millions and millions of gallons of dark, rich crude spewed into the thin atmosphere of Mars and quickly out into space. The crews tried to divert some of the normal flow away from the ruptured pipe and a *second* disaster fell upon them. The diversion pipe burst as well and even more oil escaped into the skies. *Al Quæda* sabotage was immediately suspected, but insiders could not figure how their imagined militants would have gotten to Mars to create the problem. Nevertheless, it was leaked to *Fox News* that it was definitely the work of Osama bin Laden's grandson. Well, they report; you decide.

When they heard about this rupture, people on earth couldn't understand why this was a problem. Such breaches had happened many times on earth, but oil didn't go into space, it just stayed on earth to pollute streams, beaches, oceans and the fish they ate. It stayed put, where it was supposed to be. But the gushers on Mars were a different kettle of fish. Because of the thinness of the Martian atmosphere the oil spurting out into the air formed golf ball-sized globules that drifted out into space, much like people had seen space-walking astronauts drift while repairing the many space stations around Earth.

Whether Hummericans understood the physics involved or not; they were about to feel the effects of this massive leak. Back on earth the sun's rays grew dimmer and dimmer and the polar icecaps grew bigger daily. The oceans were visibly dropping. One reporter thought he had a Pulitzer when he reported on the first sighting of the top of the Golden Gate Bridge in the receding Pacific Ocean. Flying over the area in a *News 7* helicopter, the newsman announced that he thought he could also see the Transamerica Pyramid Building just below the surface.

But for the Hummer Corporation the chilling temperature was only a minor problem, like a head cold to a person with cancer. This was because their profits came to a tire-screeching halt. Hummers eat gas like giraffes eat grass. No grass and giraffes die. No gas and Hummers look silly and useless.

Seeing all the idle Hummers people in the USH began to question their necessity. One daring newspaper headlined: *Why can't we have fuel-efficient cars like the Europeans?* Hummer Corporation goons showed up in the middle of the night and bashed the newspaper's computer system to bits. Other newspapers reported the crime the next day without asking any silly questions.

Some people had hoarded gasoline and were able to keep their Hummers going for a couple of weeks beyond the advent of the disaster in space. But once reserves were used up, the sixty-nine point nine percent of the Hummericans with Hummers parked them in their driveways. Some of the non-Hummer-using population kept putting along a while longer, but they too eventually were brought to a halt. Hummericans didn't know what to do, but some felt that their government had led them down the proverbial primrose path.

In a fit of non-strategic thinking, the faux President of the USH, who was also the CEO of the Hummer Corporation, then declared the strategic reserve of gasoline and diesel fuel held by the military to be available to anyone with a Hummer, but not to those still rolling along on non-Hummer wheels.

It was then that the EU, under the leadership of the CEO of the Volkswagen Corporation, invaded the United States of Hummerica. They quickly destroyed the gas guzzling Humvees and M-25 tanks of the USH army, which were sitting vulnerably with empty gas tanks. Volkswagen had been innovating for years with smaller cars and alternative fuels. Their planes, tanks and armored vehicles were attacking the USH using batteries filled with wind-powered electricity and hydrogen-powered engines.

Apparently, victory doesn't always go to the biggest, ugliest guy on the block.

****

The longer story is a cold one. The Ice Age descended on victor and vanquished alike, Hummericans and Europeans. Space became so polluted with oil globules that repair personnel could not go to Mars; nor could those on Mars get back. They died there. Many on Earth began to die of the cold too. Since Earth's precious petroleum resources had been squandered by America and other nations suffering from affluenza, there was little fuel to heat homes in the winter months. Antarctica grew larger, engulfing the bottom third of Latin America. Glaciers covered all of Canada and the northern states in the USH, which had now become a colony of the EU. In Europe, the Aletsch glacier in Switzerland expanded to gigantic proportions, as did those in Austria, France, Russia, Iceland and Norway.

Where they could, people flocked to the tropics, but territories there had become very cold as well, though not as frigid as in the regions closer to the expanding polar ice caps.

Then, rather fortuitously for Humankind, an Italian scientist named Immacolata Di Giovanni, working alone in her laboratory at the University of Milano, made the needed breakthrough in hydrogen fuel production. Her research allowed the manufacture of enormous amounts of fuel at near zero cost. Her discovery enabled Earth's inhabitants to tap the energy locked in the planet's most plentiful resource: water, most of which by then was frozen. Hummers and rocket ships alike could now operate using water or even garbage as fuel. Anything and everything became fuel, thanks to her research. An entire town could be heated for a year with the energy locked in a single tree.

The year's garbage of a place like Cincinnati could be converted into enough energy to heat every home in Ohio for the next century. Since hydrogen fuels were non-polluting and since humans could now actually convert garbage into power at nearly no cost in dollars, euros or yen; for the first time since the Industrial Revolution, Humankind had at its fingertips the possibility of cleaning up the planet instead of soiling it.

At first, it was slow going. The necessary production facilities had to be constructed, tested and so on; but eventually, though not until countless millions of people had died, European plants began to churn out unmanned space vehicles fueled by hydrogen power that were dubbed "scrubbers." They could fly through space and "eat" the globules of oil that were keeping the sun's rays from reaching earth, taking the oil into themselves, converting into further energy and continuing on.

Mars had long before stopped spewing its petroleum into space and after some years the sun again began to shine normally on earth. Humankind began to rebound and human beings went right back to their old ways. Capitalist production began to disgorge an enormous quantity of consumer goods and people clamored to buy them. Nations made war on each other, people made love, dogs barked and it all went back to the same-o, same-o.

Except for one thing: Hummers were optional.

5. Blood on the Tractor

Kajia-Bein and the elders trekked to the White Man's relic, the old rusted tractor, almost lost in the tall, parched elephant grass at the edge of the village. It was an annual trek.

The Harmattan winds, Africa's hot, arid scourge of the dry season, blew viscously against their faces, making their minds confused and tired. Every year, during the season the missionaries call Christmas, the wind started in the torrid Sahara, rushing southward across desolate shifting dunes, where it picked up fine sand, funneled it skyward, forming slate-colored clouds, at times blocking out the sun. Moving across the Sahel, the wind maliciously deposited its cargo of dust on the lives of all below. A thousand miles to the south, after losing much of its gritty burden, the wind still had the power to sandblast the mud huts of the Sisala of Northern Ghana.

Kajia-Bein wondered if the ancestors were listening. Each year they made the pilgrimage to the shrine. Each year, the White Man did not come. Kajia-Bein wondered why. The White Man had saved them once, from Babatu and the slave-raiders. Then he had promised progress, a new life — tractors, fertilizer, new seeds. Kajia-Bein had thought life would change, become easier. But then the first tractor broke. No one knew why. One day it just stopped. The fitter from town said it needed petrol. They tried that. The tractor was broke. The fitter came to the village and looked at the tractor, its plow still sitting in the uncompleted furrow. He tinkered. He fidgeted with the wires and levers. Finally, he shrugged his shoulders. The tractor was broke, he said. He didn't know why. Perhaps the White Man knew why, but the White Man had gone away. Far away. No one knew where.

Kajia-Bein and the elders squatted near the old rusty tractor. Some of the younger men began to clear the grass, in preparation for the sacrifice. Someone else produced a kola nut. When it came to Kajia-Bein, he took a portion, placed it in his mouth, and began to chew. He chewed and thought of the White Man and his promises. He thought of his forefathers and wondered if they were still alive in death, as the Sisala believed. Why hadn't the White Man brought the promised goods? Why didn't the ancestors go tell him of the misery in the village? Why didn't the sacrifices work, year after year? Kajia-Bein was running out of hope.

"Maybe the rains will be strong this year," someone said.

Kajia-Bein pulled his cover cloth around his frail body, tighter against the wind.

"Only god knows," someone else replied.

Kajia-Bein spat a stream of red kola juice on the dusty earth. Neither god nor the White Man seem to care, he thought.

"Last year's rains were very weak," said the first elder, stating what everyone knew as a fact.

Kajia-Bein saw the White Man's relic was now exposed, ready for the sacrifice. He removed his cover cloth from his bony shoulders, tying it around his waist. Then he took the calabash of millet water in his left hand, the chicken in his right, and squatted before the tractor, which loomed above him, as it did every year, a reminder of the fading promises of the past.

Perhaps with less relish than he had invested before, Kajia-Bein said the prayer, asking for the White Man's tractors to return, supplicating the ancestors' aid in bringing back the magic of the White Man, his power, his promises, the assurance of a future implied in his words. Kajia-Bein asked for help from the sky god, his messengers, the spirits, the farms, the sacred crocodile pond, the shrines, the cosmic powers of *yapring*, the deep bush.

As he spoke he dripped a portion of the white milky liquid on the faded green fender, the tropical sun having worked on the lush industrial color which had seemed so bright and promising when Kajia-Bein first saw the tractor coming into the village — so many years ago.

When the millet water was finished, Kajia-Bein took up his knife. The chicken, perhaps sensing its end, struggled in his grip, but with an experience movement Kajia-Bein drew the blade across its throat, holding it above the fender of the White Man's tractor, its life draining on the metal in hopes of renewal.

When there was enough blood on the tractor, Kajia-Bein threw the chicken into the dust. It flopped and twisted about, till it, like the tractor, which had sucked away its life, was dead.

Kajia-Bein spat out a stream of red juice, not meaning to hit anything, but the spittle hit a passing dung beetle, who, in his surprise, flipped onto his back. Kajia-Bein squatted down to examine the beetle. As the others drifted away listlessly, Kajia-Bein wondered if the beetle would ever right itself, or would it die there in the hot, dry dust of the Savanna. A slow, bewildering death. In the shadow of hopes.

6. *Fun Under Tarps*

We thought we were studs, Reggie and I. We liked to chase girls. We thought we were unique. We thought girls didn't chase us. We thought we were the chasers, not the chasees. We got caught as often as we could. We thought we were special. We were so young we didn't know girls had needs too. We thought only guys got horny. We were horny stupid guys, about girls at least – both ways, horny and stupid.

But we were deeper than just getting laid in the back of a '49 Ford. Actually, any model would do, cars that is – though the girls had to be classy. That's what we always said. We had standards. And we were deep – intellectually so. That's what we always told ourselves, Reggie and me. We thought we were especially deep because we liked to fish and ski. We were well rounded, we thought. We hadn't been to college yet. When we went to college we realized we had some rounding to do, not the backseat of a '49 Ford kind of rounding, but in other things – books and ideas and that kinda stuff.

In time we got really well rounded. But when we were young we were just happy to think we were studs, albeit deep thinking ones. You've probably figured out that we just thought we were deep thinkers. We were young and we did foolish things. We didn't do much deep thinking when we were drinking or skiing.

Like the time we drove four hundred miles drinking single malt whisky from Styrofoam cups in the pickup's pullout cup holder. We kept the bottle hidden in case of cops. We were lucky as well as stupid. We didn't see a cop till the end. The end came somewhere in the rain in a ditch in Montana. When Reggie tells the story these days, now that we are old and *really* well rounded, he calls it a barrow pit. At the time I thought it was just a ditch. In any case, I was lost, down a dirt road and couldn't find our camp. The three-point turn didn't exactly turn out the way I had planned. With my butt-end down in the ditch or barrow pit or whatever it was, we were not going anywhere.

We didn't spill any single malt whisky though because none was left. I think that might have been why we were in the so-called barrow pit. We sat there and laughed for a while and then I had a so-called idea. I thought I would get out and put the damn truck in four-wheel drive. I couldn't do a three-point turn and now I want to attempt four-wheel drive. Whisky, single malt or otherwise, can do that to your thinking. The four-wheel drive thing seemed like a good idea at the time but I hadn't taken all the factors into account that we needed for success at three a.m. on a rainy night somewhere down a dirt road in Montana.

What I hadn't taken into account was the physics of my getting out of the truck with way too much single malt whisky in my legs and I also had not planned on the slant. Pretty soon, as I was falling backwards, my mind figured out the slant problem, but my legs were too drunk and they let me down. Hard. On a rock hard. I think it was not only my legs that were drunk because I didn't get up and say ouch when my head hit that rock. I think my head must have been drinking up some of that single malt whisky that went to my legs. That's what I was thinking, lying there in the rain. I was thinking ouch but I didn't say ouch.

Reggie was thinking too. He was thinking I was prostrate in the mud in the rain lost in Montana. He covered me with a plastic tarpaulin. He was my friend. We chased girls and fished together. But we shouldn't have been drinking single malt whisky driving through the rain in Montana. Or anywhere else. We got wiser later when we became better rounded. Back then we were lucky and stupid, but the luck part won out.

I don't think the tarp he threw over me was very thick because I could see the cop's flashing lights through it. Its little holes and webbing produced a kaleidoscope of colors flashing all red and blue and I lay there thinking it was the Fourth of July in the middle of Montana at three in the morning. My mind and legs were inebriated and I was laying very crooked – on a slant. The next thing I remember was a Montana-looking cop pulling back the tarp. He must have wondered what I was up to under that tarp, way out in his state, lost up a dirt road and with my pickup truck parked funny. He looked down at me and simply asked: "Sir, have you been drinking?"

At the time this question struck me funny, but I didn't laugh. Reggie and I have laughed about it many times through the years, but we didn't feel like laughing then. There was a tough-looking guy in uniform, with a gun and lots of flashing lights going off in the middle of nowhere. It wasn't our turf.

I think we were stupid and lucky guys. I know we were lucky because this really rugged looking policeman let us go. He must have been going home or on the way to visit his girlfriend (we have come up with a number of theories telling the story over and over again). In any case, he just told us to sleep there for the night, slanted in the barrow pit and to go find our camp in the morning. It seemed like the best idea I had heard all night and I thought of how to thank this scary Montana cop with a big heart, but by the time I got my thoughts together he was gone. His girlfriend must have been awfully pretty. Or horny. I hope both.

We actually caught some fish on that trip, after getting out of the barrow pit, though not right away because of the really bad headaches we had. Must have been the altitude, don't ya think?

Next we tried skiing. We liked skiing because we could chase girls very fast, doing really stupid tricks on two pieces of wood and all the time hoping these antics would get us laid. We were still stupid and on this particular day we weren't so lucky. In the middle of a really girl-catching stunt, Reggie broke his ankle. High on the mountain and low on the ankle. The low-on-the-ankle-break hurt so much that Reggie howled and bawled, lying in the snow high on the mountain. I mention that it was high on the mountain because that is what we college educated, well-rounded people call a cogent fact. You will see its cogency in a minute.

Being high on the mountain, it took the ski patrol a long time to reach us. Someone had to ski down, then they had to ride the lift up and then they had to find us. We were just two dark dots on a big white mountain. Reggie was lying in the snow not thinking about doing any more stunts to catch girls. He was howling and wailing.

He was still screaming when they covered his face with a tarp and strapped him into a toboggan. When I looked at the mummy that had been my friend I thought to myself: *I would not want to ride down the mountain in a toboggan with a tarp over my face.* I was right to think that, as you will see in a moment.

I was reflecting on another tarp moment in the barrow pit when the young ski patrol guy reached for the safety strap to attach to the mummy who was my friend. As he turned his head to get the strap off his belt, my mummy friend started off down the mountain – alone.

Now I don't know where they get these ski patrol guys, but I out-skied him easily chasing my friend the mummy. Unfortunately for Reggie, neither of us was good enough to catch a free wheeling sled heading straight down a double black diamond run. I don't know the speed the mummified projectile reached but it certainly came to a very abrupt halt when it got to the parking lot. Against a VW bus, with hippy drawings all over it. Had there been any girls watching this unique way of handling a double black diamond run they might have been very impressed and the mummy might have got laid that night.

When I finally got down the hill and pulled back the tarp, it didn't look to me like Reggie was thinking about getting laid. As I stared at his ashen face, all I could think to say was: "Sir, have you been drinking?"

7. The Cat Bag

The anthropologist finished writing his ethnographic notes for the day. The candle had melted down to a nub and it was time to crawl under the mosquito net, grab an Agatha Christie mystery and lock Africa out of his thoughts for the night. But something Bubachebe had said earlier in the day stuck in his mind. Bubachebe was his gawky, big-eared field assistant. He had been helping the anthropologist build the evening fire and the sun was setting over the Savannah. Looking up at the setting ball of fire, enlarged as it dropped to the horizon, anthropologist had casually commented: "Wow! What a beautiful sunset." The remark was offhanded, not even meant for Bubachebe's elephant ears.

"Saah, you are a strange one," he heard Bubachebe say, almost under his breath.

The anthropologist straightened his back, standing up from the hearth, the evening glow fading around him. "What do you mean, you little witch?" They had developed a joking relationship over the years they had worked together. The anthropologist was using the term *hilla*, which meant witch, normally a term one would never use when addressing another tribesman. Bubachebe almost always addressed him as Saah, imitating the fawning Africans of the colonial period who had frequently jumped to the beckon call of the White Man by responding with their accented, Sir!

"Saah, you white people are so strange. A sunset cannot be beautiful. A girl can be such or a cow, but not a sunset."

The remark had stuck in the anthropologist's mind and had prompted him to write a couple of pages in his journal on cultural differences in perception, which had led to thoughts of art and how different peoples must necessarily express their view of the world in distinct ways.

Tired now of the day's fieldwork and the oppressive heat of the March day, he lifted the mosquito net from the straw-filled mattress and crawled in. He found the paperback under his pillow, tucked in the net and struggled to read the page in the diffused light of the flickering candle, coming in as it did, faintly through the mesh of the mosquito net. The anthropologist tried not to think of tomorrow's sorrow. It was to be his last day with his tribe, the people he had been studying for over two years. He would leave the village and its good people behind and journey the hundred or so miles to Bolgatanga, the nearest city with cold beer, refresh himself with a couple of days stay in the old hotel left over from the days of White rule. He would continue south by Mammy Wagon, crossing the Volta River by ferry and then on to Accra and the plane that would take him back to England and to his college at

Cambridge University. The candle flickered and sputtered and went out, the light leaving his hut like the fading sun that had triggered the exchange with Bubachebe.

The anthropologist lay there in his tiny enclosure, in the darkness of the African night. He would miss it all. These villagers had become his friends. He had been given an African name, a kinship status in the lineage of Fuojang. He had found a place where he was liked and he felt close to the Africans of his village that he had never found, even in his small hometown in America.

He put down the novel and began to fall asleep, the sadness coming over him like a blanket. As he drifted off he was saved, however, from becoming too morose by his cat, a black and white beauty, which cuddled up to his backside and purred. It was their last night together too, he thought.

He and his cat, named Marx, had been constant companions during his time in the village. Marx had been given to him shortly after coming down the dusty path and taking up residence in the backwater they called Bujan. ☐The big man of the village, who they called Teacher Salifu, had brought it as a welcoming gift, just a tiny ball of fur, not long away from its mother's teat.

The anthropologist fell asleep trying to remember the good people like Teacher Salifu and his other research assistant named Marifa Kanton and most of all, the bright boy he had taken as his adopted son, Nenkentie. He tried to concentrate on how he had grown to love these people when sleep blanketed him and he floated to another realm.

☐* * * * *

The next morning the anthropologist was busy with preparations to leave. He had packed his knapsack and loaded the saddlebags on his motorcycle. He was prepared for the long, bumpy, dusty, hot ride and hoped the bike would make it to Bolgatanga without breaking down. He was worrying about the bike's staying power when old Tiawan sidled up to his hut door, as he commonly did, begging for this or that. Tiawan was the senior elder of the village, the *Nihiang Nihiang*, but for the anthropologist he had been a pain in the butt. Not only was he a cranky old man in his seventies; old for this part of Africa, but he was an inveterate moocher. He would try to sponge something off the anthropologist almost every day.

Tiawan had been the one villager that the anthropologist had always tried to avoid, but like the proverbial bad penny, he always seemed to turn up when an interview was in progress, or when he and Bubachebe were making dinner. Today was to be no different. The anthropologist was busy with last minute arrangements, using the early morning hours to get ready for what would be a long and tiring journey and there stood Tiawan in a ragged old blanket, even though the heat of the morning indicated that the dry season day would approach 120 degrees Fahrenheit.

"What do you want old man?" asked the anthropologist, irritated at the interruption.

Tiawan didn't notice that he was being bothersome. "I was wondering if I could have your cat. You can't take him on that motorbike."

Now the anthropologist was irritated with himself. He had misjudged Tiawan apparently. The anthropologist leaned back in the rocker outside his hut and smiled. "Well Tiawan, I didn't realize you were an animal lover." The anthropologist was speaking their language and had incorrectly used the term for a sexual lover.

Tiawan guffawed. "You can love a woman, but you can't love a cat."

Nearby, helping with the anthropologist's preparations, Bubachebe snickered and said: "You White People are so strange."

"Stop bugging me, you floppy-eared witch," joked the anthropologist. "Get the man his cat."

Bubachebe obediently retrieved Marx from the hut and handed him over to the *Nihiang Nihiang*. Tiawan took the cat in his gnarly hands, turned abruptly and walked away without another word. Ungrateful bastard, thought the anthropologist.

"He doesn't love your cat, not the way you do," warned Bubachebe.

"Don't worry about Marx, just get that stuff boxed up and take it over to Teacher Salifu's hut. I'm giving his wives all those blankets and stuff."

"Big deal," Bubachebe said sarcastically. The anthropologist ignored his remark and continued to sort through the items he would leave behind, thinking who would get what. The morning continued in this manner until it was time for him to get on his cycle and head for the city. Several villagers came to say goodbye, some giving him pito beer to drink, others bringing him slices of cooked yam and other foodstuffs.

As he had mounted his motorcycle and cranked it up, the anthropologist noticed Tiawan coming his way. *Begging to the end*, he thought.

But Tiawan proudly extended his knobby hands with a parting gift. It was a black and white fur bag, which had been sewn in such a way as to include Marx's startled face.

8. A Call from Iraq

The telephone call came in the middle of the night, when the evening's drink hadn't yet worn off, but the deepness of sleep had overtaken the day's worries. I hadn't had enough of either drink or sleep to handle what I was to hear on that call. It was my son calling from the battle of Fallujah, the first one that took place in Iraq in November 2004.

Let me give you a little background on myself. I do this so you will understand how deeply this call affected me, though no doubt you will think that it probably would have devastated almost any parent who got such a call. It was something short of two uniformed Army officers showing up at my front door - the visit that every parent dreads when they have a son or daughter fighting one of our country's wars, but it was almost as dreadful.

I am a retired college professor who went to college in Berkeley during the 1960s. I went through the Free Speech Movement there, thought the world was quickly moving toward peace and freedom, listened closely to the words of the Beetles' songs to find some meaning in life and, of course, I marched against the war in Vietnam.

Oh yeah, like most of my friends and colleagues I smoked those funny, hand-rolled cigarettes that took a person to another dimension, but through the years I got tired of them and switched to fine wines from the Napa

Valley. All that is to say I mellowed in some things but held on to my anti-war stance.

I know being anti-war is about as fruitful as being against mosquitoes. Both kill, but both are damn hard to eradicate. I read in one of Kurt Vonnegut's novels that some movie producer once asked him what kind of a book he wanted to write and Vonnegut had answered: an anti-war book. The producer, who must have seen way too much of life by that point, answered: you might as well write an anti-glacier book. Well, we're doing in the glaciers a lot faster than war. So it goes.

So some forty years after marching in protest of war, with people spitting in my face while waving the American flag, I get a call from a son who insisted to fight for his country.

Apparently he had talked a reporter into using his satellite phone and here I was talking to my son with the sounds of battle going on all around him. I could hear machine guns and an occasional louder blast, which my son later told me came from RPGs - Rocket Propelled Grenades. Whatever it was, none of it sounded like a place I wanted my son - or any other son, for that matter - to be. Yet here I was talking with him in the middle of a terrible battle in a faraway land in another questionable war.

My son was in CyOps, which is Army slang for Psychological Operations. When he told me he was going to Iraq and that this was his MOS, I envisioned him dropping leaflets from a plane or sitting far behind the lines writing inane propaganda for the locals. He wasn't so lucky. He wound up atop a ill-equipped Humvee manning a fifty-caliber machine gun and wearing forty pounds of body armor in one-hundred and forty degree heat. He said is was so freaking hot that you drank your required bottle of water every hour and never peed.

At first he got to ride around an Iraqi town where most people waved and smiled at him and he thought war was a piece of cake, even if he was an obvious target for some insurgent sniper. He gave away candy, took photos posing with guns and tanks and stuff. It all seemed unreal, or that's the way he conveyed it to me in an occasional email.

The phone call was something else. He was crying and one phrase from that night stands out in my mind: "Dad, I got more war than I bargained for." Haven't we all, yet it was relatively easy for me to be against war, teaching at posh American universities and living the good life. My son was in the middle of hell and had just had a buddy blown to smithereens. The Marine had taken an RPG shell in the chest and even a Kevlar jacket won't repel that. As we spoke he still had his friend's blood and pieces of his body all over his helmet and body armor, even on his face and hands. He, his fellow squad members and an NBC correspondent were momentarily pinned down by sniper fire and he had not had a chance to wash the horror away.

I couldn't make out everything he said because the connection was not that great and the movie-like sounds of war in the background would occasionally drown out what he was saying. But I knew he just needed to make contact with someone or something that was not part of the hell around him.

He said that they had been at it for several nights in a row. Their job was to drive their Humvee through the streets of Fallujah with loudspeakers playing obnoxious music to cause the "bad guys" (as he called them) to shoot at them. The enemy fire would produce flashes and flares in the night and then the Marines would be able to pinpoint them and return fire more effectively. "I'm a bulls-eye, Dad," he said, "a sitting duck."

But apparently, from what he told me that night, being a target atop a hunk of slow moving metal was not the worst part. The Marines who were their backups came under very heavy fire and it was necessary for my son to get down from the Humvee and fight with a rifle door to door. Press reports said that U.S. soldiers had not had to fight in this way since World War II.

My son told me that he was scared, which seemed perfectly understandable to me. But what was very interesting about holding a gun ready to kill another person was that my son didn't want to do it. He said his greatest concern was that he might kill an innocent person who just happened to walk around the wrong corner at the wrong time; or that he would kill a fellow soldier. Apparently soldiers carry their humanity into battle, like a flak jacket or sidearm. Fear of being hurt and fear of hurting others seem to be standard issue.

My son survived Fallujah, in a physical sense anyway. He didn't get killed, he didn't lose a limb and his fear that he would kill someone else didn't come about. But he didn't entirely escape the horror of war.

I've been telling you about a call from Iraq, which to me was extraordinary. To think that a modern-day soldier could call his father from the battlefront certainly bears out the fact that we have made technological advances as a civilization. Of course, we would be far more civilized had there been no battlefront, no need for the first telephone call.

But I want to tell you about the second call. This time I made it to my son. I placed it to his home here in the states and did so, without realizing it, on the anniversary of the beginning of the battle of Fallujah. My son was so drunk that he could not talk very long with me and our conversation had to be continued in a third telephone call, after he had sobered up. In the few words we did exchange in that second telephone call he briefly explained that the thought of Fallujah's horrors had come to him many times since leaving Iraq, but it had been especially difficult on the anniversary of the battle, which had been on all the news programs and in the newspapers. What was merely information for the average viewer or reader was, to my son, a returning veteran of a troubling and horrendous event, a stimulus to his posttraumatic stress.

After the second phone call I came to understand that war stuck to my son in the battlefield, not exactly like the pieces of his friend's body. Those he was able to remove and eventually wash the Marine's blood from his hands and face. There was some other terrible residue of war that adhered to my son and secondarily struck at my heart and more importantly, his. And that residue he could not wash away, not even with alcohol.

9. *A Fallen Friend*

I hear that an old friend had died. As I know I will be in the neighborhood, I stop by and console his widow, who also is an dear friend and very smart lady, one who had turned an ancient farmhouse and the yard into a slice of heaven.

It is a warm Wisconsin day when I arrive at the entrance to the farm. I pull my rental car off the highway into the drive and see the great red farmhouse, the lush gardens, the fountain spouting mists of water in the air, the magnificent oak tree and the run-down barn in back. I know that there are trout swimming in the pond out back.

I ease the car up the driveway and park at the backdoor, which is about the only way anyone visiting the Hudsons ever enters the house. All of their friends are backdoor friends and there are many of them. The Hudsons are the kind of wonderful people to whom other people of value are drawn. They enrich the lives of everyone they meet. I was fortunate to have been introduced to them and the memory of my time with them pulled me through many doldrums between the time I last spoke with them – some forty years before – and my visit now.

Fran is at the kitchen window and comes out to greet me, wiping her hands on a dishtowel, though it is clear that she doesn't recognize me. We are both much older. However, she and Fred are accustomed to a variety of people dropping in to visit and to pay a kind of homage to them, as many people feel as I do, that Fran and Fred Hudson are at the top of the list of marvelous people in the world.

When I say my name Fran breaks into a broad smile. She remembers me after all these years. We hug and say the things people say when they have been apart for a long time, but remember each other fondly.

Then we go into the kitchen and she shows me a vase I had given her many years before. I don't remember the vase, but I don't let on. She goes on and on about the vase and how every time she puts flowers in it, she thinks of me.

While she is going on about the gift, I see Fred asleep on the couch at the far end of the living room, which is open from the kitchen. I feel an electric shock go through my body. My mind goes numb. *Fred is alive!*

I see that Fran has stopped talking and is looking at me in an odd way. There is puzzlement on her face. I realize that I am staring at my sleeping friend. "Are you felling unwell, Sam?"

"Nuh…no. F…Fred"

"He has good moments and bad, but that's to be expected at ninety-eight, don't you think?"

"Ninety-eight?" I stammer stupidly.

"Last week. The fifth. Wants to make it to a hundred he says, but now he sleeps a lot. I'll wake him."

"No, no. Don't. I can come back another time."

"Where do you live now?"

"California."

"And you're here for…?

"An art show in Door County."

"Better see him now. At our age you never know." She smiles broadly.

"Really…" I start to say, but Fran walks through the dining room, past the great fireplace and to the couch in front of the bay window that looks out on Lake Winnebago. She wakes Fred, saying: Sam Mendes is here, hon. Remember Sam?"

The ancient man, my old friend of so long ago, pulls himself upright on the couch and that old familiar crooked smile spreads across his face. It is an impish smile that always makes Fred look like a schoolboy about to pull off a monumental prank.

I am home. I know we are going to pick up exactly where we left off. We sit and talk and Fran disappears into the kitchen. She is making tea, which she knows I like at any time of the day.

Fred and I talk about the past, the state of the nation, which we agree is not so great, and many things. We are happy. I know I am and I assume that Fred is because that wonderful smile never leaves his face. He is young again in our friendship.

Fran seems to be gone a long time, but we push on covering a myriad of subjects, knowing we have only a short time together. We both want to make the most of it.

After some time I see that Fred is tiring, so I say that I am going to see what's keeping the tea. I get up and so does Fred, but he is wobbly and teeters before me. Then he falls forward into my arms. My friend is very heavy and I instinctively bend my knees and arch my back to keep us both from falling over.

I hear footsteps behind me and I shout "help me!"

"What's wrong Sam? Are you hurt? Are you in pain? You're standing awfully funny."

I begin to ease Fred back onto the sofa and fall forward landing on top of him."

"Yes, you better lie down for a minute. You look like you've seen a ghost," says Fran holding two cups of tea in her hands.

Quickly, I roll off the couch and jump to my feet. I don't want to hurt my old friend. But I sense that something is wrong. Fran should be very concerned about Fred and she is just standing there smiling and holding two cups of steaming tea.

"I...I..."

"Sit down on the sofa. Relax. Here, drink this. It'll make you feel better. You're quite pale."

"But what about Fred," I sputter.

She looks at me askance. There is a long pause and then she says, "I guess you haven't heard. Fred passed away last week. The fifth, to be exact."

10. A Painter of Note

The parrot had entertained us many times through the years, my hubby and me, usually after a breakfast shared in the sunroom, his cage being just off that nook. He would listen in on our conversations and then repeat certain words and phrases, sometimes in my feminine voice; at others in Jim's voice. We thought he was cute. That was before he became critical of paintings.

I have to tell you a little bit about myself to make you understand how this green and red bird became an art critic – and more.

I am a well-known painter who works in oils and pastels. I sell in many galleries in the United States and am well respected abroad too. But more than being just an artist, I have been teaching the subject for about thirty years. I have developed a large following of devoted students and teach classes that are usually arranged by others in various locations throughout the world.

Recently, as I am getting on in years, I have wanted to hold more and more of my workshops in my large studio, which is attached to my New Mexico home. I have a close friend who owns some guesthouses nearby and I put the students up there and some in my own guesthouse. The money is better, since I don't have to pay a middleman, and my friend makes something off the rentals. Most of all, however, it cuts down my time on the road, which can be tedious, traipsing all over the world with painting paraphernalia, some of which is difficult to get on a plane in this crazy post-911 world.

Anyway, the last workshop was going fine, with my students painting and with me observing. Sometimes I go around and make suggestions, even show a brushstroke or two for a student who is not too touchy about having me alter his or her "masterpiece." At some point in the workshop, however, we move to a group critique. I put all the students in a semicircle and have each one in turn put their paintings on a demonstration easel for all to evaluate.

Often we paint *en plein air*, which is outdoors, but on the occasion I am going to tell you about we had poor weather and needed to paint indoors. One student in particular wanted to try to paint my parrot, whose name is Pedro. I was not too sure about him as a model as he moves about in his cage so much that it becomes difficult to draw him effectively. Nevertheless, I knew that he would remain relatively motionless if I took him out of his cage and put him on an open-air perch. I put down some white drawing paper to protect the carpet and got Pedro situated on the crossbar of a demonstration easel above the protective white sheeting.

Most of the students were thrilled to have a "live model," though I am sure the men in the group wanted a different kind of "liveliness." In any case, they each began to paint Pedro in all his feathered luster. For the most part he was motionless, only moving his head from time to time to preen himself.

Each of the under drawings proceeded well, except for Alfred's effort. He just couldn't seem to get a handle on the right proportions for Pedro. As the other painters were already laying down paint, Alfred moved ahead without getting his parrot well drawn. I heard him exclaim a couple of times about the "damn bird" and such.

At the end of the exercise we formed our usual semicircle and each student put their painting before the group for an analysis of their progress and to receive any tips on how to proceed or correct any mistakes. As each student placed a "parrot" in front of the group the real Pedro seemed pleased and continued to whistle or make little clucking sounds.

But when Alfred put his canvas up on the demonstration easel, the petulant bird stopped preening himself, fluffed his feathers so as to make himself appear bigger than life and said, in a loud voice imitative of mine: "Shit!"

Amid the roars of laughter in the studio that followed this feathered critique, Pedro once again puffed himself and would have been smiling broadly, if parrots could smile. In all his puffiness, he let out a greenish-blue stream of critical feces that hit the white paper on the floor with a splat and splatter. In fact, it made one of the better abstract paintings ever produced in my studio to date.

Pedro had made the rather dicey transition from being merely an art critic to becoming a painter of note.

11. *The African Songbird*

My driver pulled the Land Rover up to the South African/Moçambique border crossing and I got out amidst Africans going west meeting Africans going east, some coming from months at labor in the mines – others returning from extended vacations at home in the former Portuguese colony. I stood in the shade of a tree listening to the birds singing, while my driver arranged the formalities of my visit.

On the road again inside the war ravaged landscape that looked like a bombed out Beirut without the buildings, my driver pulled off the road, or what had once been a road, and drove through the bush beside it. We kept about a hundred yards to the south of the east/west road as we headed for Maputo, the jewel-like capital of Moçambique that had been called Lourenço Marques in colonial times, indeed since Portugal invaded the place in the 16th century.

My driver kept an eye on the bombed out tanks and armored personnel carriers that stuck out like craggy dead dinosaurs along the roads, some of them left among the bomb craters in the roads, others strewn by the wildness of battle here and there on the roadside. They were our beacons keeping us going in the direction of the capital city – ghostly reminders of the mayhem that wracked this country in a fifteen-year ideological bloodbath over two foreign ideologies: Communism vs. Capitalism.

As the five hours of our bumpy journey dragged by, I had time to contemplate the effects of war and compare it to my many journeys through Africa elsewhere, some through old Biafra with its bombed out buildings and bullet-ridden mud walls; others through streets with this-ethnic or that-ethnic blood still visible on the streets; but many more expeditions through more tranquil countryside, where nature had made the holes in the road and where tall red, jagged anthills were my guides. I had time to wonder if the thousands killed along this road had really understood the history of imperialism that led to their deaths, to destruction so devastating that all the birds actually left Moçambique. I wondered because, as we drove for hours through the bush, we never saw a single village, a single native, a single animal, nor did we hear the birds sing. We were driving through Africa and on such a drive almost anywhere else on the continent, one dodges mothers with babies on their backs and loads on their heads; donkeys with their burdens; pilgrims going hither and thither in search of salvation; traders hawking their wares; or simply children playing in the road. In Africa, the driver usually has to dodge life, not reminders of death. In the Moçambique of the 1980s, it was the reverse.

We drove through an eerie landscape of madness and only saw one signpost of sanity, a single inkling that Humankind might still have a chance at a coupling of civilization and modernity. That was a soldier guarding a communications tower, which stuck up high above the silent birdless forest, humming its modern song. Below the blue-helmeted UN peacekeeper just gazed at our Land Rover as we bounced by. We waved. He waved. And I continued to wonder – what has happened to Africa? Why is there so much more of this kind of Africa now? Would there be more in the future? Was this some sinister portent of Humankind's fate? One has time for such ruminations on a trip through the ashes of hell.

We finally reached the bombed out buildings of Maputo and put up in the gleaming golden tan hotel by the sea, which was under renovation due to war damage. Perched above the warm waters far below, it was still a stalwart reminder of glorious days of the imperial past in Lourenço Marques – that is "glorious" if you weren't African and didn't know of a future without the bird's song.

As we had first approached the palatial edifice amidst the palms, I noticed the signs of war on the faces of gaggles of young men who stood aimlessly on the street corners, smoking nervously, looking furtively about, as if in search of a future beyond the gun. Almost as if still clinging to their sweaty khaki clothing, the sounds of a forest war were echoing in the air, the last shrill sounds of violence.

As my driver and the hotel valet were dealing with my bags, I stood under the swaying palms, in the shade, out of the intensity of the African sun. The afternoon was silent. Too silent for Africa. Yet I could hear the wind rustle through the fronds above. I could hear the ocean lapping on the rocks below. As a *costeleto perdido* of Portugal, I wondered if my ancestors standing in this place had heard the song of a bird. Mendes. Silva. Costa. Vaz. Mendonça. Had they heard the birds sing as they set history in motion in this land, so far from their native Portugal? Would they have forged ahead if they knew of a scorched land ahead, one with no songbirds.

"*Ja está*," said the porter. The room was ready.

As I began to move from the shade, a street vender approached and blocked my path, as if to tell me something. I looked at the urchin. He was smiling the smile I had seen elsewhere in Africa and I looked at his only ware – a caged songbird.

12. The Pig Farm

She wasn't the most social of persons. A self-proclaimed ar-*tist*, she mostly stayed in her bungalow by the river. She was also known, by the few who had actually seen her, as an eccentric dresser – Anne Hall hats, wild, fluffy scarves, loose-fitting blouses and ankle-length skirts that never matched, but they were always brightly colored. Bird and flower patterns were her favorite. She was never seen to wear shoes, sun or snow.

There wasn't much going on in the sleepy little valley and, consequently, she was a focal point of gossip. She usually held the floor for at least an hour in the never – ending tittle-tattle at Emmy Bensen's bridge social, which was faithfully held every Wednesday morning (nine to noon, call if you can't come).

If she was a recluse, she had picked the right spot. On the north was the un-crossable river, which butted right up against the Sangre de Cristo Mountains, home only to mountain goats and elk (and other critters she didn't want to know about). On the west were heavy woods, which probably had more things that prowled in the night. On the east lay a hundred acres of undeveloped pasture and tall grass, small trees and brush. No one could see her from three directions.

Her only crack in the armor was the south side of her tiny piece of property. There, her land butted up against the two-lane highway that ran into town one way; and off to the city on another, which fortunately for her, was fifty miles away. She solved the problem with a high fence and a locked gate. She couldn't get it high enough to be entirely safe from view, but it kept most people out and that was the best she could hope for. Besides, across the highway were nice looking mountains with pine trees that she liked to look at from her kitchen window.

The joke in the valley was that the rare pale-headed brush finch was seen more often than this peculiar lady. Gossips pondered and postulated about what the inside of her house must look like. With no evidence, they assured one another that it was a mess. It was whispered that she was probably "a bit off."

When the land developers came, opinions changed.

It happened one Monday morning about ten o'clock. A black Humvee with a yellow real estate logo pulled up in front of the hundred-acre plot on her eastern flank. Two men in business suits stood on the side of the road and pointed at the land and talked, then pointed some more.

She watched them from her kitchen window. *What are they up to?* She knew it was not a good omen. Men in suits never were. Men never … (well, that's another story).

When the men in suits drove away, she made a strong cup of Irish Breakfast tea. A good cup of tea was her solution for most of the planet's ills, which, since she had no television or radio and never read newspapers or magazines, was quite a small world. But it had ills, like two men in dark suits. Two men in her life, even at a distance, might warrant two cups of Ireland's second favorite drink. She filled the teapot to the brim and set it to boil. *Why were they pointing at that deserted land?*

Her little world got rattled a week later when the same black Humvee showed up, but this time followed by a pickup truck with worker-type men in jump suits. She watched from her hideaway as they unloaded big plastic boxes that, on the sides, said: *survey equipment*. They drove into the field and opened them, taking out tripods and telescopes and long orange lines wound around stakes.

This does not look good, she thought. *This amounts to an invasion.*

The reason the valley folk had to reevaluate her mental competence is based on what she did next. Oh, she didn't do it while the men were there. She didn't even do it later when they returned and went into the field and staked it out, sighting this way and that with their grade lasers and level rods. She didn't do it when the bulldozers came and leveled a gaggle of house pads.

She did it when they had finished marking out each house site, when each pad had been given some individually in the envisioned subdivision and when the suits returned and put up a huge for sale sign that said:

"Forward View Subdivision – Half Acre Lots for Sale."
She had a sudden flash vision of two hundred home s
adjacent to each other and, more importantly close to her,
right next to her hideaway.

It wasn't a professionally painted sign, even though
she told someone once that she was an accomplished oil
painter. In fact, it was crude, or they were, because she
made twin signs. They were identical twins because they
both said the same thing: PIG FARM in red letters on a
gray background.

Carefully, she erected the lies so that one faced the
road and the second faced east. Anyone driving up could
see the sign in front and once they turned into the proposed
subdivision they could also easily see the second sign. PIG
FARM. Two lies, but effective fibs.

The two men in dark suits couldn't sell a single plot
in the envisioned subdivision. Zero out of two hundred.
That's not good odds in the real estate business, so they
took down their "Forward View Subdivision – Half Acre
Lots for Sale" signs and went away. They never came
back, but eventually the brush and tall grasses did. With
time, even some small trees began to take seed.

But she left her deceitful PIG FARM signs up – just
in case.

The valley bridge aficionados had something new to prattle about, but no one ever called her dense again, that quirky lady with the PIG FARM *sans* pigs.

13. *Compartments of the Mind*

My dad and I were hunting on old Fred Hamn's farm. The sun was already down when I saw the pheasant – a brightly colored cock. It was just a silhouette against the dark orange horizon. It was probably illegal to shoot it in the pale evening darkness, but there was no way I was going to pass up the opportunity. It was my first pheasant with my new four-ten.

My hand was shaking when I raised the barrel and took aim. What I remember most, after all these many years, is the flash of fire coming out the end of the shotgun. And then I was running toward the flip-flopping bird. In my insecurity as a hunter I was sure I had missed the bird and it was just flapping around out of fright. I thought it would get away and I would have to deal with a great disappointment. I didn't like being disappointed when I was ten or eleven or whatever I was at the time.

But I had killed the magnificent painted male, with one BB in the throat. I didn't tell my dad that only one BB had found its mark, out of the many in the shotgun shell. I probably had aimed too high or too low, but I grabbed my prize by the long and only slightly bloodied neck and held it high.

"I got it dad! I got it!"

That night in the bar my dad owned I was the center of attention and a hunter was born. Everyone said it was the biggest or the prettiest or the nicest cock pheasant they had ever seen. It sure was to me and again I failed to mention that I only hit it with one out of many BBs.

It has always been easy for me to find some fault in success, a negative trait that has dogged me throughout my whole life. To this day I remember being ashamed that all the shot didn't find its target. I've kept quiet about this fact all these years, part of a little mental compartment of kid-shame hidden somewhere deep inside.

Later, when I was a student in college, in that same secreted compartment I filed away the disgraceful B minus I got in English (and me a writer – imagine!). The C in some other forgotten class took up even more space in the shame compartment.

It didn't matter that all my other grades were A-minus or better and that I graduated *Summa Cum Laude* and went on to become an anthropologist with a Ph.D. from a famous European university.

It seems that that shame compartment is bigger than the fame compartment.

As a kid I wanted to be a great hunter. I read stories by Zane Grey and others about hunting and survival in the wilderness. I lived on the Sacramento River whenever I could, with my gun and dog. I ran a trap line along the river, tanning pelts of muskrats, beaver and fox. I fished endlessly. I identified with outdoorsmen who wrote of the adventures in *Outdoor Life* and other such "manly" magazines.

Maybe that's partly why I eventually went to Africa and lived in an isolated village deep in the bush in Northern Ghana. My rural upbringing certainly served me well there, for one of the first questions the village men asked me was: "Are you a hunter?"

The elders asked me this for a couple of reasons. First, I had brought along a shotgun, one of the few in the tribal area, most of the hunters there were still using old blunder busts left over from the slave wars. They were not very accurate and unfortunately exploded from time to time. The men were very taken with my shiny single-shot twelve-gauge.

The second reason they asked me if I was a hunter was that hunting and manhood were strongly connected in that culture. When I proudly replied that I had been shooting animals since I was a kid, they seemed pleased and, unbeknownst to me, set up two tests to see if I really qualified as a hunter. The first came about when I was invited to attend a sacrifice on a male hunting shrine, a simple conical-shaped mud mound with Eland horns sticking out the top. The rite took place in the inner courtyard of a hunter's compound, where he and the other men of the village sat around in a circle. I was given a chair as a sign of respect, while the others squatted or sat on low stools. Looking around, I could see that the outer walls of the hunter's house were covered with skulls and horns.

In time a dog was brought forward, its throat was cut while the hunter called on his ancestors to help him have greater success in the hunt, its lifeblood drained into a large calabash, which is a bowl made out of half a gourd. When the blood was about finished spurting and draining from the jagged gash in the dog's neck, the man holding the body placed it momentarily over the altar, dripping a few last red drops on the shrine's horns. Everyone shouted *Janwo*! I was told this meant: So be it, or something like that.

Then came the test. The calabash of frothy blood was handed to me and I was told that every man who was a hunter, most of whom were in attendance, had to drink of the dog's blood to insure that all the village hunters would have luck. "If you are really a hunter," one young man said, "you must take part in our ritual, just as you will participate in our hunts." There was a look of anticipation on their faces as I stared at the bowl of blood, which by now had more than one housefly struggling in the crimson foam. The older men were grinning widely, as most of them had known white men in colonial times. None had ever seen a white man drink blood. I was the morning's entertainment.

By this time in my life I wanted to be a good anthropologist more than I wished to be a great hunter, but the two pursuits had congealed in the warm calabash of blood in my hands. Not wishing to appear unmanly, I quickly put the container to my lips and drank. Actually I *appeared* to drink more than really ingesting very much blood, but I made sure that I drank loudly and got lots of the red stuff on my lips and chin.

Everyone seemed pleased. I had passed my first test. Maybe I wasn't the Great White Hunter of my youthful reading, but I was a White Hunter to them.

That night I got test two. I need to explain that hunters are thought to be the most macho of men in that tribe because hunting is best done at night, deep in the bush. The African bush contains two kinds of dangers – imagined and real. The tribesmen think that evil spirits live in the bush and that they are especially menacing in the dark. Only a "real man" would venture out of the village's circle of safety after sunset.

Secondly, nighttime in the bush means walking amongst dangerous animals – a hyena alone can bring down a man and break his neck in a heartbeat – and also there are two-step snakes. These are nature's little wonders that impart venom that paralyzes their prey's nervous system. One bite from these little guys and you drop dead – one step, two steps. Dead!

I had anti-snake pants, khakis with double-thick legs; and the natives did up their shins with wraps of cloth to make protective leggings. But we all kept a watch out anyway, using miner's headlamps to light our way when possible.

The hunting party assembled at the chief hunter's compound around midnight. It was a jovial group, many of whom were fortified with native beer, some with *apeteshi*, which was a form of what they call white lightening in the Appalachians.

I was stone sober and apprehensive. Going out on Fred Hamn's ranch with your dad at sunset hunting birds is one thing; venturing into the "Heart of Darkness" with a bunch of drunken guys carrying highly combustible guns is another. And we weren't bird hunting. We were after big game, animals that could fight back, especially in the dark.

As we waded through the tall grass, the natives were always stopping and staring up at the trees. At first I thought they were trying to see the outlines of roosting Guinea Fowl, but they told me they were looking for "gorillas." As one who had read quite a bit on the flora and fauna of West Africa, I knew the closest gorillas were hundreds of miles to the east, in the Congo. However, we did hear some of these guys and I assumed that they were chimpanzees from their hoots, which were familiar to me from television programs. Also, since I always paid top dollar for bush meat, hunters would bring me the smoke-blackened bodies of these all-to-human looking animals to buy, but I always passed. Duikers and antelope were much more appetizing.

After spending several hours staring into the trees and traipsing through elephant grass over our heads, we heard a noise, the sounds of the first big animal of the night. I had to take the shot and I'll have to explain why. First, I was being tested, though I didn't know that at the time. Secondly, the one or two hunters with shotguns were not about to waste a shell that cost a day's wages on anything but a standing animal. This animal was crashing wildly through the underbrush. Since everyone turned their headlamps in the direction of the sound, we could get a glimpse of yellow-flashing eyes, almost neon-like, bouncing along, disappearing behind logs and trees at times, but indicating the path of the animal.

"Go ahead Salia," they said, using my African name. "You get him."

I didn't know what the "him" was but I raised my gun and pulled off a quick shot, with more reaction than plan. The fire that leapt out into the African night took me back to Fred Hamn's farm and another kill with my dad. This time it was not a pheasant, but a wolf.

After I fired the crashing stopped. Everyone ran to the spot where the eyes disappeared and there was the "him," a shaggy dog-like creature, white teeth snarled in a last grimace of pain and fear. It was one of the luckiest shots of my life and it earned me the reputation of a great hunter – a "real man."

Later I bolstered that reputation by shooting partridges out of the air, which no one had ever seen done before. People told stories about me and women made up songs that are still sung today at festivals, chronicling my great hunting feats and some that I never did (but who am I to correct them?).

The problem I had with the killing of the wolf was this: there was no blood on the animal. *Had the damn thing died of fright?*

The natives were thrilled at having some meat to bring home, but as they turned the body over and over they kept exclaiming: "No blood. No blood."

The head hunter, an elderly but robust man, stood up at looked at me with awe in his eyes, which I could see in the glow of our miner's lamps. Clearly he was astounded. Someone muttered the native word for magic. A craggy elder's eyes said yes – strong magic.

I figured the creature had died of a heart attack or hit his head on a log while fleeing, but I wasn't about to turn down more machismo, for I had learned enough about these people to know that in addition to the linkage between manhood and hunting, there was a strong association between being a strong man and having magic. If I was going to live there for a couple of years, I wanted to be considered a strong man.

I kept my mouth shut.

My assistant hoisted the dead animal on his head and we returned home. It was light by the time we reached the village and deposited the carcass on my front porch. As the boy dropped the dead animal on the pounded clay floor, I noticed a tiny drop of blood splatter to the hardened earth. I knelt down and inspected the animal's head. There it was. I had brought down a forty-pound animal with a single BB, which caught him just behind the ear.

I was puzzled. *How could that be? One BB?*

As I stood there trying to figure out how I had killed the wolf, a crowd gathered and the chief hunter began to explain to the villagers that this Great White Hunter had killed the animal with magic. I caught the words: "mighty strong magic."

I thought of the tiny spot of blood on the neck of the long-dead pheasant and of the shame I had at making a less than perfect shot on Fred Hamn's farm. I put my foot over the spot of blood on the mud floor and twisted it and the red became brown, absorbed by the earth.

I thought about the night's events for a moment. I saw the newfound respect in the eyes of the crowd of villagers and decided to put this one, not in the shame compartment, but rather in the fame compartment.

14. The Sleeper

The teenager was to be the ultimate sleeper. He would help with their plan to bring America, *The Great Satan*, to its knees. He was to be the central player in the Master's long-term strategy to infiltrate America's political structure at the highest level. The Master knew that Allah is patience personified.

Chosen because of his wealthy and well-connected family, one that already boasted two Presidents and several congressmen, Jimmy Thrush was being groomed to sit behind the desk in the Oval Office. *Allah has time.*

His trainer had stopped by the tent to say goodbye to their new hope, this skinny rich kid who had unexpectedly fallen into their hands, who had voluntarily come to the Middle East to learn Arabic, enthralled as he was with the exoticism he found in books about the region. He had trained well, taking to the *Qur'an* like a true Arab, like a son of Mohammed.

His trainer hugged Jimmy, lavished him with praise and kissed him on the cheek, three times – right, left, right. "You go into destiny – your fate is the will of Allah. *Allah a akbar.*"

"*Allah a akbar!*" replied little Jimmy Thrush with a certain amount of gusto.

* * * * *

Ashanti Washington stepped out of the Oval Office, leaving President Jimmy Thrush behind, alone at the well-known teak desk. He was signing more papers and talking on the phone at the same time. *And they say he can't walk and chew gum too*, thought Ashanti, who had changed his name to Wilson, partly to make his Afro-centric parents angry and mostly to enable him to get to the top of his profession. He hadn't thought Ashanti would quite cut the mustard in the Secret Service. In any case, with lots of hard work, he had risen to the top. He was part of the President's personal staff, a highly trained bodyguard.

Wilson leaned against the wall, smiling. Inside he could hear the President speaking, though it was not easy to make out the words and, in any case, that wasn't part of Wilson's job. He didn't play politics. He never purposefully listened in on the President's conversations, phone or otherwise. He would protect any President no matter his party or politics. However, Wilson *was* wondering why there hadn't yet been a black President or a woman in the Oval Office when he heard President Thrush speaking in what sounded like a foreign language. *A foreign language!?* The thought rushed into his head: *The guy can't even speak English well.* Intrigued, he leaned closer to the wall, near the crack between the door and the well-oiled walnut frame. He was sure that the President could not speak another language, his lack of knowledge about things overseas being legendary. What he didn't know was that that feigned ignorance had all been part of the Master's long-term strategy.

In fact, Jimmy Thrush – now President Jimmy Thrush – had always been an avid reader of history and geopolitics, but as part of the Master's strategy, he read in private and in public he appeared to know just enough to get him elected at each point in his climb to the top.

Wilson could hear more clearly now. *He's speaking Arabic! Or is it? Some language like it anyway.* Wilson strained to hear the words, but the President apparently had his back to the door and was speaking in hushed tones.

Then the bodyguard heard the impossible: *"Allah a akbar."*

God is great? In Arabic? Can't be! He listened with all the intensity he could muster. Wilson figured he had misheard. Surely the President of the United States could not speak Arabic and moreover he would not say something like that. *My God, he's the darling of the religious right!*

The sound of conversation continued, but now quite muted. Wilson looked up and down the hall. Nobody. He leaned close to the walnut frame, putting his ear to the crack. Just before he heard the distinctive click of the President hanging up the receiver Wilson Washington heard it again: *"Allah a akbar."*

"What the hell am I supposed to do with this?" Ashanti "Wilson" Washington was talking with his beautiful counterpart, one of the most gorgeous white gals he had ever seen. Wilson had "fallen" the first time he saw her, but nothing had ever happened. Professional ethics and all of that.

"Come on," said Natalie, "you must have this one wrong. *Allah a akbar?* That's *Al Quœda* talk."

Natalie Swain was Wilson's junior partner, but she liked him right off because he never treated her like a subordinate. She enjoyed being around him too. He was the best at what they did and she could learn a lot from him. Then there was the fact that he was a hunk. In fact, he put Denzel Washington to shame. *I wonder if they are related?* But she tried not to think about that. They both could definitely fog her glasses.

"I heard him say it, Natalie. Plain as day. I couldn't hear the other stuff, but he ended the conversation with *that* phrase and he said it with conviction – a little louder."

They were having coffee at the Berry British Teahouse near the White House. Lots of the Secret Service folks hung out there. "Well, if that's the case.......if he really said those words........" Natalie was searching for the right phrase.

"Exactly. How do we explain it? It doesn't make sense. The President speaking in the enemy's tongue? This is crazy." Wilson found it difficult to keep his voice down. His emotions were flowing and his mind was abuzz. He straightened up and looked around the room, as if looking for the answer in the crowd.

Natalie wanted to reach over and take his hand, but she merely said: "You know, we have an obligation to report this."

Wilson swung his head back: "Yeah, I'm gonna go upstairs and blurt out that I heard the President of the United States, Mr. Jimmy Thrush, who can't seem to get his English grammar straight, speaking Arabic on the telephone. C-1 will laugh me outta his office."

"Okay, I see your point, but what should we do? This isn't in the training manual anywhere."□

Wilson let out a tiny laugh, the tension easing out with the sound. "Yeah, its not every day you might think the President is cavorting with the bastards who pulled off 911."

"Is that what you think, Wilson? Really?"

"Natalie, I just don't know what to think. Sometimes I think I misheard him, but every time I go back over the words I could pull out of the garble, the conclusion is the same: I heard the guy say it – *Allah a akbar*."

They sat in silence for a while, their tea getting cold. Then Natalie asked: "What about the tapes? They would have caught everything."

Wilson had forgotten that Congress had mandated taping of all Oval Office conversations, in fact, most everything that took place in the White House. Part of the post-911 homeland security push. "Yeah, the tapes!" He slapped the table so hard he spilled his tepid tea. "We gotta get the tapes."

Natalie wiped up her spill with a frilly napkin that said: "I luv Britain on it." "Where are they? Where do they keep the recorder, or whatever it is they use?

"I'm not sure, but I think it's in the basement in the homeland security room. It's a secure six room."

"Are we cleared for that?" asked Natalie.

"Don't think so. Secret Service at our level goes to four."

"Who can we get with a six clearance? Who can we trust?" Natalie was leaning across the table, her body tense.

Wilson fidgeted with his cup and saucer. "There's really nobody I can go to with this thing. It's too weird."

They looked at each other, thinking along the same lines. Eventually, Natalie said it: "Wilson, we have to black bag it, don't we?"

"Or back away. Maybe he said something that sounded like *Allah a akbar*. I mighta misheard him. I could be wrong." Wilson raised one hand into the café air, a sign of despair.

"And if not?" continued Natalie. "What if the President of the United States was actually speaking Arabic? What was that all about? Even if he was speaking Arabic, it might be innocent. Who was he speaking with!? We gotta tell someone or do something." She was saying this softly, into her teacup, trying to convince herself as much as Wilson.

There was a long silence while the two professional bodyguards, members of the special unit to protect the President, were contemplating a felony. They were trying to get their minds around breaking into a secure room in the White House basement, the very thing they were hired to prevent, among other things. They were risking their careers by even talking about it. In silence, each fought mental demons. Without spelling out the details, each one came to the same conclusion: they had to break into that room. They had to know what was on that tape.

* * * * *

When Natalie and Wilson were on the same shift and when it was over, they met in the basement coffee room. It was normal for people to congregate there and kibitz after work, drinking coffee, flirting or just unwinding from a grueling, tension-filled day. Unlike the others in the little cafeteria, Wilson and Natalie felt the tension rising. They were winding up, not down.

"Are you sure nobody's in there now?" asked Natalie, anxiously.

Wilson set down his cup. "Should be all clear. No one is assigned to that room. It's more of a storage room. Once in a while, the taping system gets checked. The maintenance chart is on the door, where the guy signs off. Looks like he goes in there once a week, maybe to change the tapes. I don't know."

"Have you got the picks?" Natalie said this in whisper.

"Yeah," replied Wilson, trying to think about what this might mean for them, not the danger, not getting caught, but for them. As a couple. *Can we be a couple? She probably doesn't think of me like that. Yet, sometimes……the way she looks at me………*

"You're stalling Wilson."

He smiled. "Yeah. This is scarier than taking a bullet for the Prez."

They giggled nervously, like kids about to break an adult rule.

When they had finished their coffee and most of the people had wandered off, the two made their way down the hall to the room that held the taping system. It was locked and the chart on the door indicated that the maintenance man would not make a visit till Thursday. It was Monday.

Natalie watched the hallway while Wilson picked the lock. They both were trained to do this and had the appropriate tools of their trade. It was an easy lock and the door swung open gently

After looking both ways, Natalie put her hand on his shoulder and said: "All clear."

They slipped into the dark room, closed the door and flicked on the light. One whole wall was covered with an elaborate network of tape machines and wires and what looked like a stereo system and speakers that the Rolling Stones might use.

"Christ, what a set up!

"Your tax dollars and mine," replied Natalie sardonically.

"Where to start?"

"There must be a log or something. What day was it you heard the President?" asked Natalie, pragmatically.

"Last Thursday."

"Time?

"Well, I took the box of papers into him at 2:30. I remember checking my watch. So it was just a few minutes later."

"So we look for the tape between 2:30 and 3 p.m. on last Thursday."

Wilson began to search the drawers of the cabinet holding the machines. One held pieces of wire, a few tools and some staples along with their staple gun. Another had various kinds of tape – masking, electrical and that really strong stuff people used on packages.

While Wilson was rifling the drawers, Natalie went to the computer console in the center of the mess of wires and screens. When she hit the space bar, a screen came up with a gold background and several icons. One said Oval Office. She double-clicked on that. "Wilson, check this out."

"Whataya got?" he said, closing the last drawer.

"Looks like it's not a tape recorder, not one that uses tapes anyway. It's all digital. It's here in the computer system. Here's the schedule." She showed him a screen with dates. "There's Thursday the 14th. There's our baby." Natalie clicked on Thursday the 14th and another sub-screen appeared. It had two twelve-hour clocks, one for a.m. and the other for p.m.

Carried away by the beauty of the technology, Wilson said: "Cool," momentarily forgetting the gravity of their actions.

Natalie double-clicked on the two spot on the dial on the p.m. clock and the President's voice began to play over the speakers.

"Yikes, that's loud. Can you turn it down," asked Wilson, anxiously looking at the closed door, as if armed guards were going to break in any moment.

Natalie found the little icon that looked like a zipper and moved the button in the center to the right and the President's voice faded. She found a level that they could hear, but wasn't loud enough to be heard through the door. "Better?"

"Yeah, okay but that's not what I heard."

"No, that's 2 p.m., before you arrived with the papers." She clicked on 2:25 and the speakers crackled with background noise and sounds of papers shuffling, perhaps a pen scratching on paper. More crackling sounds and then a knock on the door.

"Come in," the President's voice.

"Here's the papers, sir." It was Wilson speaking. "I brought them over from the Capitol. The box is secure, Mr. President. No funny stuff inside."

"Thanks, Wilson. Nice to know it won't explode in my face, though what I have to sign might."

They both laughed weakly and standing listening, the two voyeurs also laughed nervously.

Then there was the sound of Wilson's footsteps, the door opening, the door closing. More paper shuffling. More crackling sounds and what sounded like the President moving his chair. One of the hinges apparently needed some oil. Then a phone ringing and a clicking sound. The speakers went blank. No sound came out, not even crackling.

"What?" exclaimed Natalie.

Wilson straightened up. He looked at the speakers and he knew: "The bastard switched to system off."□

"Son-of-a........." Natalie quickly clicked on 2:45 p.m. and there was the Thrush's voice in English talking with someone about a thousand dollar a plate fund raising dinner. He was trying to shorten the time he had to be there and apparently the person on the other end was trying to negotiate more of the President's time.

"It skips," said Wilson, stating the obvious. "He turned off the conversation in between."

Natalie clicked out of the screen and put the computer to sleep. "Well, that's our answer. He didn't want anybody to hear what he was saying."

"Or how he was saying it," confirmed Wilson.

"He didn't want Congress listening to the President of the United States speaking to someone in what must be pretty good Arabic. What the hell is going on!?"□

"Look," said Natalie, turning away from the computer screen, "there must be some reasonable explanation. If he speaks Arabic with someone, maybe it's just a friend. Maybe his friend doesn't speak English. It could be all very innocent."

"Then why turn off the tape? Why hide the fact that he speaks Arabic? Have you ever seen any press release or media report on the President speaking Arabic? That would be all over the headlines, given the fact that people make fun of his lousy grammar and his c-minus grades at Harvard."

"Okay, okay. I agree. Something is not right here, that's for sure, but let's get outta here. We can talk about it at my place. We both need a drink."

* * * * *

Wilson was impressed with the neatness of Natalie's apartment. He made a mental note to clean his before *ever* inviting her to his place. He hoped he would get a chance to do that someday soon. He was getting to like her more and more and what was even more important was that he was feeling comfortable around her. In good moments, between thinking about the insane situation they found themselves in, he thought she might like him too.

Natalie poured out two Dewars, one with no ice, the other with a couple of splashes of water. They sipped them and went ahhhh and enjoyed a moment before having to again turn their attention to what seemed like a national security threat.

Wilson broke the silence. "You know just speaking Arabic would not have done it for me. You could explain that. There are lots of reasons why he would keep it a secret and he could have been talking about any number of things that do not threaten our country. What with 911 and everything, he could have just wanted to play dumb about being able to speak the enemy's language."

"But the tapes," Natalie interjected.

"Yeah. Why did he turn off the tape if it wasn't something sinister? That's the corker. Or is it? I dunno. Maybe he just didn't want Congress to know of his linguistic peculiarity."

"Sooooo …….. what do we do about this, if we really think there is a threat?"

Wilson shook his head. "I don't know, I really don't. Maybe we should take this to C-1 now that we've got him turning off the tape while speaking with someone in Arabic. Maybe we should kick it upstairs."

"We'd feel awfully silly if it turned out to be nothing. Maybe we'd get canned. We did break into to a secure six facility."

Wilson nodded in agreement and took another sip of his scotch. "We have to find out more about how and why he speaks this language. Hell, most Americans can't remember twenty words in Spanish even if they took it in high school. And the media is always harping on Thrush's bad grades. He couldn't have been much of a student. How'd he learn Arabic of all things?"

"Maybe he lived there," Natalie threw out. "Perhaps he was a foreign exchange student to Saudi Arabia or someplace like that – somewhere in the Middle East."

The night went on like that, back and forth, both uncertain as to the proper course to take. Finally, after much debate and a couple more drinks they decided to look into the President's past, make some discrete inquiries about his early life. It seemed the prudent thing to do. If they found some innocent reason why America had an Arabic-speaker as a President, one who apparently didn't want anyone to overhear him speaking the language, then they could back off and no one would get hurt.

* * * * *

Wilson had some time off coming and went to La Tuna, Texas – just outside of El Paso. It was the hometown of Jimmy Thrush and Wilson wanted to talk to some of the townspeople to get an idea if, as a young man, Thrush had ever lived elsewhere, traveled a lot – Wilson didn't really know all the right questions to ask, but he planned to start somewhere and see where it took him.

He was registered at the local Days Inn and let it be known that he was a reporter and that he was doing a book on La Tuna's most famous son. It was a good cover, since such strangers popped up from time to time, doing research for this or that story on the President.

On his first morning in La Tuna, Wilson took a stool at the counter of Mabel's Cafe, which seemed where most of the good ole boys of La Tuna hung out. Mabel was in the kitchen and from what Wilson could see of her through the opening in the wall, she was a black "sistah" and living large. However, besides Wilson, she was the only other "colored" in the joint.

Most of the talk at the counter centered around farming and ranching and, of course, the weather. Some guys in a nearby booth were dressed in camouflage fatigues and were clearly coming from or going to hunt deer. The camo guys were talking politics, a variety that would have been right down Thrush's alley. *Any movie director could find lots of redneck character actors in Mabel's Cafe today and probably on any day of the week*, thought Wilson.

A girl with buckteeth and a pink uniform poured Wilson a mug of coffee as he sat down. She did this even without asking if he wanted any. "Whatcha have, hun?"

"I'm going to have a couple of cups of coffee before I decide, if that's okay."

Sure, hun. Holler when yer ready." She moved along the counter's inside rail, pouring cups of the weak black coffee as she went. This sure wasn't a Starbucks.

When Wilson was working on his second cup, a farmer in blue coveralls, sitting at a counter stool on his left, said, "Howdy."

"Good morning," replied Wilson.

"Gonna be a hot one," continued the farmer, using the universal slide into a conversation.

"And a bit humid for me," replied Wilson.

"Not from these parts, are ya?"

"No, I'm from New York," lied Wilson. □"Big city fella, huh? Whatcha doin' in La Tuna?"

"I'm writing a book on President Thrush's early life, before he got into politics."

"Ha! That kid was born into politics son. Comin' from the Thrushs he didn't have a chance. First lawyerin', then takin' office. They move up the ladder from one office to anothern. All them Thrushs 're climbers."

Wilson ordered scrambled eggs and ham and the toothy girl refilled his cup for the third time. "You are sure right about that but lots of books have been written about the Thrush politicians. I want to do one on the young Jimmy Thrush, before he started to climb. Did you know him then?"

"Course I knowed him. The Thrush ranch butts up to mine. My Billy and Jimmy used to play together all-a-time. He was just a normal kid. Nothin' special, 'ceptin he was born into the Thrush clan."

"But what did he do that was different? That's the kind of stuff I need for my book. What made Jimmy Thrush "the boy" stand out from the crowd?"

The farmer turned his stool toward Wilson and said: "Well, jiz bein' born a Thrush 'round here set ya up fer that."

"I see your point, but I need details, you know, to flesh out a book you have to have facts, fine points and interesting stories about his early years." Wilson drained the last of his coffee and the waitress slid his ham and eggs in front of him and refilled his mug all in one motion. "Do you remember him traveling or speaking any foreign languages, something special like that?"

"Oh, he was odd after that trip, fer sure. He 'n Billy were like two peas in a pod till ole Jimmy went off overseas. Disappeared fer 'bout two-three years. He was different when he came back. They didn't play together any more."

Wilson finished chewing a mouthful of scrambled eggs and asked: "Do you know where he went for all that time?" He tried to make his inquiry sound as innocent as possible.

"Eggs easy, sweetie. My usual," said the farmer to the pink girl, who flashed her bucks at him and slid along the counter pouring.

"Overseas. Europe and the Middle East, I think."

Slicing into the ham, Wilson asked: "Do you know why he went?"

"I dunno. Jist to git experience I guess. With the world, ya know. Part of the plan."

"Plan?" □

"To become governor, then President. That was the plan when little Jimmy popped outta his mommy's belly. He hit the bottom rung of that political ladder runnin' fer office." The farmer laughed at his own metaphor.

"Europe I can understand, but why the Middle East?" Wilson really didn't know what to ask next. He was fishing, but didn't know if he was casting into the right water.

"Well, ya see, little Jimmy was like my Billy in lotsa ways, but he was always a bit different. 'Tween you 'n me, maybe a bit strange even."

"Strange? How?"

"Read books all the time. Got all caught up in Arabs and Camels. Had some Frenchy guy, the one that wrote that book *Madame Bovary* I think. Read all about his love of Egypt. Kinda identified with 'im, I guess."

"Gustave Flaubert," supplied Wilson.

"Yeah, some Frenchy like that." Jimmy read all his journals 'n stuff. Was obsessed with A-Rabs and such."

Wilson had read about Flaubert's love of the Orient as it was called then in a marvelous little book by Alain de Botton called *The Art of Travel*. He finished off the last of his ham and pushed the plate away. "So the young Jimmy fell in love with camels and pyramids and stuff like that, just like Flaubert?"

"Yeah, he was always readin' anythin' he could get his hands on 'bout rag-heads 'n such." Wilson was unfamiliar with the term rag-head, but he figured he knew what the Texas farmer meant by it. The N-word in cloth.

"Well, that *would* make a La Tuna boy a little different from most kids his age, I guess." Wilson really didn't know the proper direction to take the conversation.

"Different? Hell, he was strange inside his momma." The farmer was going to stick with his metaphor. "But when he ordered them camels – well, that's when I knew he as a little – ya know, teched in the head."

"Toy camels?" asked Wilson innocently.

"No, not toys – the real thing. Real shit-dropping camels. Can ya imagine? Camels in Texas." The farmer guffawed. "Brought 'em over from Arabia or some such place over thar. Use-ta dress up in them funny robes, ya know and rode one or another'n a those camels all over the ranch. Even came over ta my place one day ridin' one a them crazy things. It actually spit at me."

The rest of the conversation remained fixed on the strangeness of little Jimmy's obsession with all things "A-Rab," especially the spitting, stinky, cranky camels that he kept in one of the Thrush barns. The farmer couldn't offer much more information about the nature of Jimmy Thrush's trip abroad other than he was gone a long time and came back changed somehow. More interested in climbing on that political ladder, the farmer said. Dedicated, he was.

"Seems like he had a plan," said the farmer as Wilson bid him farewell.

"Looks like it worked," Wilson said, moving toward the door.

"Yep, put little ole La Tuna on the map, he did."

* * * * *

Natalie sat down at the breakfast nook in her Washington DC apartment. She poured her morning cup of tea – Earl Grey, with a pink packet of sweetener. She read the back page of the *Washington Post*, then turned to the other stories, turning the pages slowly toward the front page, which she liked to save till last. It was a quirky habit she had followed since childhood. She always read a newspaper or magazine from back to front. When she was about half way through the *Post*, she shrieked and spilled Earl Grey all over her bathrobe.

What had startled her was a small story in page A-5. It read:

> La Tuna, Texas. The local sheriff of La Tuna Texas today reported finding the battered body of a Washington DC resident, Ashanti "Wilson" Washington in a back alley of this town. Mr. Washington was a Secret Service agent, working in the White House. The President issued a statement saying that his staff members were all saddened by the death of Mr. Washington who had been a valuable member of the White House personnel for the last eight years. Apparently Mr. Washington was in La Tuna on vacation. Speculation has it that since he was of African-American heritage, the killing may have been racially motivated. Police are continuing the investigation. A former Marine and a member of the Secret Service, Mr. Washington is to be buried here

at Arlington National Cemetery with full military honors.

Natalie was stunned. She slowly rose from the table, in a daze. When she spilled the tea she had thrown the newspaper down and now she saw the headline. It read: *President Thrush Threatens Israel with War.*

America has certainly changed, she thought absently.

The lead story went on to explain that, somewhat surprisingly, President Thrush was the first modern President to withdraw America's traditionally strong support of Israel and throw the weight of the White House behind Saudi Arabia, which, in recent years, had increasingly come to support the Palestinian cause.

Natalie was staring down at the newspaper when she heard footsteps behind her. She didn't have time to turn, however, as the bullet tore through her tea-soaked bathrobe and she fell dead, covering the news of the day, as reported in *The Washington Post*.

15. Two Kisses

The old man leaned on his cane, watching the approaching double-decker bus, red as they had always been on his many trips to Britain. He was at a loss for words, with her at his side after so many years. Her nearness brought back the memories of another time in London, when they had shared a night of love, back then, when he was young and strong and full of himself.

Now the body had failed him and he no longer thought of women in that way, though their beauty did not escape his eye. And she was no longer the beauty she had been, standing there softly holding his arm as the bus came to a halt before them, the conveyance of their final parting. Surely he would not get back to London and more to the point; she would never come to America. Their moment of passion had come and gone, in a capsule of a slow, youthful time, so long held in memory; but out there somewhere, a chance lost.

"Well, I guess this is goodbye," he said embarrassed at the moment.

Her birdlike face caught the morning's sun as she smiled up at him. "Not goodbye. I have a feeling we will meet again. Soon I hope." There was no certainty in his words, but their was compassion, a certain warmth.

The mammoth driver in her elevated perch looked out the opening door, waiting on the old man. The bus hissed and moaned, as if it was alive and impatient, glowing hot and crimson in London's morning sun.

The old man put his cane tip on the first step and turned to say something, but she put her tiny hand to his mouth and leaned forward. Lightly she placed a kiss on his cheek, above the white beard that covered most of his face.

"Come in sir," insisted the driver. "Got to make schedule, you see."

Startled by her last minute show of affection, he felt her release his arm and he stepped up onto the noisy bus, both decks packed with all varieties of humanity, a cacophony of languages creating an encapsulated world of noise in the bus's innards.

The old man turned to see her once more, thinking that their brief reunion had been all too short and very different in her London flat with her long-time husband sitting uncomfortably in his leather chair, smoking his hand-rolled cigarettes.

Back then, in their salad days, in her smaller flat, they had been alone and lusty in their mingling.

But now she was gone, or perhaps she was still there in the dazzling morning light. But he could not see her anymore. He was frozen by memory in the entryway of the bus, holding feebly to a fading image of her.

"Step up lively now, luv." The driver had already put the bus in motion; the sound of the door squeaking shut behind him.

The old man moved carefully to an open seat by the window. He sat down and looked for her in the milling crowd below, but she was not to be seen. He pressed his forehead to the glass and knew he would never see her again, despite her words to the contrary. He tried hard to remember what she looked like that other time, pulling the sheet to her neck, as he waved from the door. He had been in a hurry to leave, he remembered. He had had a career to carve out.

Now in the jostling bus, his head down, he felt someone take the seat next to him. His mind jumped back and forth, thinking of her then and again, as she had been moments ago. He could feel the lingering kiss on his cheek, the lightness of her hand on his arm. He could also remember the passion in that London flat long ago, his mind jumping unstably over a forty-year crevasse.

The bearded young man who had taken the adjacent seat settled himself in and said: "It's a bright one today, isn't it?"

The old man raised his head and looked at his fellow passenger and was startled. It was like looking in a mirror, but one long past, broken by time's cruel passage. The young passenger looked as the old man had appeared those many years ago when he and she had been so young and so much in love.

The young man stared at him, waiting for a response. When he got none, he repeated his greeting: "Lovely morning, for London that is."

"Oh, yes.....yes it is," the old man stuttered. "Are you off to work?" He was trying to hold on to the kiss that he could feel evaporating from his cheek as he struggled to make conversation with the young man. He didn't want it to go – the last touch of her – the last kiss.

"Work? Heck no, I'm a Yank. Just on vacation."

The old man leaned back to get a better view of the thin, young stranger, his dark hair falling over sturdy shoulders, which he held in a posture of self-assuredness.

"Yeah," the young man continued, "just in town for a few days and already met a babe. Never thought I'd make it with a Brit. They're kinda different, you know."

"Different?" asked the befuddled old man.
"Yeah, I always found it hard to talk to British girls, till last night. Met this real beauty and...... well, you know. We wound up in the sack. Great stuff too."

The mind of the old man raced back in time. He shifted uneasily in his seat, completely unaware of the other passengers around him, the rattling and shaking of the London bus.

"Oh, I see."

"Hot, if you know what I mean. Gonna go see her again this morning and get some more of that." The young man was obviously proud of his conquest and wanted to let his seat partner know that he was a stallion. "Real hottie, she was. Gotta go back to the States later today, but I told her I'd stop off and give her some more sack time. Probably won't ever see her again, but I can't miss the chance for one more lay in the hay." The young man laughed nervously at his witticism, but perhaps feeling that the old man did not understand. *He doesn't know what I'm talking about*, thought the youngster.

The old man muttered something and turned away, staring out the window at the passing London townhouses, life fluttering by in a dizzying blur. He was in another time in his thoughts but she was still with him, in that light kiss on his cheek, which was quietly evaporating as the bus rattled on. He tried to remember their passion then, back in that past London night, when *his* hair fell over his shoulders, when his tight young body entered hers. That was a time of rough and tumble sex, not of light kisses and a gentle hand on his arm. That was then and now, even though the London scene seemed so much the same, he was different.

He turned to the brash young man next to him and simply said: "Do me a favor?"

The young man pulled back. "Oh, you want me to shut up, right. Not a talker, huh?"

"No, it's not that," replied the old man, moving his face closer to the younger man, his voice falling to a whisper. "Just do me a favor when you leave your new girlfriend….."

"She's not my girlfriend, just some gal I met in the pub," interrupted the young man.

The old man raised his palm to stop the other's chatter. "Just do me this one favor. When you are through making love, when you're headed for the door, stop. Turn around, go back and give her a gentle kiss on the cheek."

"Who are you talking to, you silly old man?" asked an even older woman across the isle.

The old man looked at the woman with years carved into her face. "What?"

She leaned little closer, pointing to the empty seat next to him. "You've been talking to the air. I've been watching you. There's no one there."

16. *The Great Professor*

He was a great mind, the professor. Everyone knew that, those who were familiar with him, intimately; and also those who acclaimed him in print – reviewers and colleagues who were only acquainted with his many great works – the books, the articles – an accumulation of years of writing, thinking and publishing. People spoke of a mastermind, quietly and out of range of his hearing.

He is now gone, a genius into the mist. I heard of his death just before sitting down to write this, a kind of eulogy. A remembrance. A sadness in ink.

I remember his career; after all he was my professor at Cambridge, already a lion in those hallowed halls before I climbed the worn steps up to his massive office in St. Johns College, overlooking, as I remember, the River Cam and The Backs. Soft beauty beneath academe's hard edge.

Sometimes we would stroll along the banks, watching the students and their girlfriends, punting leisurely through the water, gliding toward adulthood in privileged gaiety. At other times we were sequestered in his cluttered office, talking of our Africa, of a shared love for the continent and its people. Anthropology was the glue of our relationship – he being the great Don and I, the fawning student.

That was back in the fog of my youth, our moments together now clouded with time's weathering. But I am fortunate to have had one more recent encounter with my beloved teacher, which occurred while I was back at Cambridge, as a visiting professor. He was there, retired but still in St. Johns, though in a smaller office, the kind they give to great men who have brought a layer of fame to the college. He had invited me for lunch at St. Johns and I found him sorting through crinkled old photos of his years in Africa, for a new book he said. Another book, his lifeblood, giving purpose. He was grayer, more stooped and, as always, disheveled. The joke in the department was that although he often came in with different colored socks; at times, perhaps when he had been thinking deeply about his intellectual labors, he arrived at work with two different shoes, one black and the other brown.

I remember seeing his frenetic figure rushing from lecture hall to office or between meetings, from one responsibility to another, through the cobbled alleyways of Cambridge with his head down, slightly bent, curly hair and beard flapping in the wind. He always had a great stack of books under one arm and his black lecture robe under the other, though sometimes he forgot to take it off after leaving High Table or when through giving a lecture. He appeared as the caricature of the mad professor and I always imagined that the music in his head, if he had any, was the equivalent of *Night on Bald Mountain*, or perhaps something by Stravinsky, slightly atonal and grating.

Those images come to me now from the distant past, of a younger teacher in a hurry. After all a career of over fifty books and hundreds of journal articles requires a certain accelerated tempo of life, a lunge at academic fame. He was in a hurry then.

In my last meeting with him, he had slowed, sitting there mulling over his past, sorting his yellowed photographs. I sat in front of his cluttered desk and waited, still his junior in years and stature.

After some reminiscing we went down to lunch, not in the formal dining hall, but in the canteen. Merle was the Senior Fellow at his college and as such he would be required to say grace in Latin before the meal in the Great Hall and, as he explained to me with a glint in his eye, he hated to do that, so we ate cafeteria-style, with less history and ceremony to our lunch.

Afterwards, we retired to the bar and had espressos, still chatting about our profession and the quirks and successes of our colleagues. Many relationships are made firmer by gossip, even in the mighty halls of academe. Neither of us was with our wives anymore, our children faded off into life's corners. I was single, firmly so; and he, faltering of frame, had taken a new girlfriend – a live-in lover. Of course this was tittle-tattle for others. We did not talk of *our* failings, but of the foibles of others, drawing closer in our sharing laughter's moment. The eccentricity of others is always more appealing than shortcomings closer at hand.

Yes, I remember this great intellect – Don of St. John's, the William Wyse Professor of Anthropology at one of the world's great universities. He was an author who left us many books and great works to ponder, but what I remember most was our last parting. We had finished our coffee and walked out into the courtyard for a short stroll on the grass, he being a Fellow, this permitting such a perk. The sun was shining and the tan stone walls glistened yellow-white in the afternoon glare. I did not want it to end, our *tête-à-tête*. You see, I had a feeling that it was to be our last meeting and I was correct, sadly so. He would die shortly thereafter, going on to be a footnote rather than a prodigious force in ivory tower life. His small office being cleared out by a college steward who may not have known the fame connected to the room's artifacts, a patina of greatness.

But sitting here now I do not remember him as a great author or brilliant lecturer. Rather, I remember his taking my hand, as a lover caresses that of another, my left in his right. We had walked naughtily over the manicured lawn, a small perquisite for two graying intellectuals, with its hundreds of years of tradition and care – the lawn groaning under passing feet. And we lingered in the sun, a rare English moment with the lawn green mixing with the sun bright. And then we began to part, pulling back, the younger and older moving away from each other. Our entwined hands raised up and our fingers began to slip away, flesh leaving flesh. I remember the feeling of loss, punctuated by a faint squeeze, an intimate assurance of his friendship. It was a small greatness, that final enfolding, that last embrace.

Today, I do not so much remember the sharpness of his mind, as the warmth of his heart.

17. Dogs and Death

When I was nine or ten years old we went to Idaho to visit my maternal grandmother, who was eighty years old at the time. I always liked visiting her, partly because she gave me a dime to chop wood for her pot-bellied stove and Montpellier, her town, smelled of coal fires, which for this California boy was a foreign and pleasant smell.

At one point during the visit my mother was alone with my grandmother in her bedroom. Grandma was in bed and not feeling well. My mother later told me that the room filled with spirits, who told her that they had come for her mother. My mother begged them to give her some more time with her mom; that she lived in faraway California and had only just come for a brief visit. The negotiation was successful and the spirits disappeared. Or, that's how my mother told the story.

The next night the whole family went to a drive in theater to see a "Ma and Pa Kettle" film. During the course of the evening my grandmother became sick and we left in the middle of the movie. Once home, grandma sat back in her rocker, which was located in the center of her living room near the pot-bellied stove. I was put in the adjacent parlor, in a sleeping bag on the floor. From there I had a view of the adults huddled around my grandmother. Some were crying and someone called the doctor. The air was filled with a strange tension that I did not understand, being a youngster.

In due course, my grandmother let out a long sigh and died. At that moment, and for many long agonizing minutes afterwards, her two hound dogs on the front porch began to wail, baying at the moon, which hung low in the smoky mist of the night sky, as the coal fires burned in most hearths, a defense against Idaho's autumn chill.

My eyes must have widened, for I remember a chill and goose bumps on my skin. The hair at the base of my neck tingled and it seemed it tightened to the point of being painful. I remember thinking: "How did they know? How did the dogs so immediately come to know that their beloved master had passed on?

It was one of my first lessons, though not fully developed at that young age, of the intimate interconnected nature of all life on Spaceship Earth.

18. *Money Trees*

I am writing a book about how rich people screw poor people. It is called *The Fabrication of Domination*.

It is a long, hopefully erudite, academic book. Few people will read it. It won't make me rich.

But I thought of a shorter book on the same subject. Maybe I would call this minuscule book something like: *Money Trees.*

The entire content would be written in eleven words:

If money grew on trees,
only the rich would have orchards.

The rich would see to that.

That would be the whole book.

Short huh?

But it won't make me rich either.

19. Surprise

Joan worked in an advertising office where everybody worked cheek to jowl, most putting in long hours. In fact, her co-workers were closer than most family members. There was only one big problem, because, as with most families, there were a myriad of smaller ones.

The big problem was that Joan was one of the most gorgeous women on planet earth, maybe in the Solar System. Of course, in an office with lots of testosterone, that would have been problem enough, but there was more to the story. Much more.

Joan worked with her ex-lover, Alexander, and for her present one, Jason. The two men even shared the Misner account, which meant that they had to work long, hard hours together, often late into the night. Both were account executives and neither was senior to the other, but they had to work very closely and Joan was the administrative assistant on that account. It was an uncomfortable and stressed troika.

Most of the time things ran smoothly, with only an occasional edgy moment, a little strain and tension at times. Then it happened.

Jason, ever the romantic, choose the Christmas party to propose to Joan. As she was talking to a group of office gals, Jason walked right up and took both her hands. He then raised them high in the air, while everybody at the party stopped talking and starred, including Alexander – maybe especially Alexander.

With hands extended in a Y-shape, Jason sunk to his knees and asked loudly: "Joan, my precious Joan. Will you be my wife?" He then let go of her hands and deftly pulled a little black box out of his shirt pocket, opened it and let it shine. It was as big as Aires Rock in Australia. The office girls gasped. The errand boy tittered.

The question hung in the air like oil fumes in West Texas, suffocating but real. Joan stood almost motionless, shifting her weight slightly from foot to foot. Her upper lip, which looked like a beautiful bird in flight, twitched. The uncomfortable stillness was becoming stifling. Throats were dry, but no one drank. Punch cups hung suspended in mid-air.

Then Joan did something unexpected, but understandable; as she had always told everyone she knew that she hated surprises. She was the kind of person that had everything in her life planned and arranged way in advance. Her desk was the neatest in the office, by far. That tidy nature was what made her an excellent administrative assistant. She ran out of the office.

When she fled the party, the air seemed to be sucked out of the room. The Christmas carol playing in the background suddenly sounded flat and out of place. The workers stood stiff and unsure of themselves. Alexander's face was the color of the Polar Ice Cap. He looked like one of those amyloidal figures in Madame What-her-name's Wax Museum. He hadn't been so befuddled since, as a lay pastor, he had to give his first sermon. Nobody said a word. Though it was Christmas, no one was merry now.

Then, just as most of the office workers were about to die of asphyxia, while the group seemed to be holding its collective breath, Joan appeared in the doorway.

All eyes were on her. Gorgeous as ever, but she seemed wracked with indecision. Her lovely features betrayed stress and tension within. The workers could see her eyes were on Jason, then they watched as she shifted her gaze to Alexander. Then she went back to looking at Jason. Then back to Alexander. This seemed to go on for an eternity, which didn't help the breathing situation in the now-claustrophobic room.

After what seemed as long as a Castro speech, Joan unsteadily moved across the room, seemingly heading for Jason, who had remained on his knees, for the lack of anything better to do. But she passed him by and went to Alexander, throwing her arms around him and bursting into tears.

Most people in the room came to know what a coronary embolism feels like; or at least the onset of a panic attack. Afterwards the office folk, men and women alike, said things like: "I felt like I was punched in the gut." Or,

"It was as

if some giant hand was choking me." And so on.

While the speechless crowd watched, Alexander guided Joan into his office, her head on her former lover's shoulder. He closed the door behind them.

They were not in there very long, but to Jason, whose blood had stopped flowing through his veins, it was a time without end. He felt like a man standing against a mud wall in front of a firing squad, while some inept Third World corporal was trying to un-jam the bolt in his ancient gun. He felt like a little boy in the first grade who peed his pants in class and didn't know whether to stay seated or run out of the room.

Crazy thoughts were going through Jason's head when the door to Alexander's office opened and Alexander moved forward, followed by Joan. They walked into the hushed crowd and right up to the kneeing Jason, who by this time had sat back on his heals, his shoulders slumped.

Joan was mostly obscured by the body of Alexander, who was a big man – much bigger than Jason. He towered over the kneeling man.

"Joan has asked me to make an important announcement," he boomed. Everyone in the room jumped and thousands of muscles twitched. The office boy tittered. Sphincters tightened.

"Joan has come to me as her pastor and asked me to preside at her wedding in celebration of her marriage to Jason."

Everyone gasped in unison. Jason's shoulders straightened ever so slightly.

Then Joan jumped out from behind Alexander with a big smile on her fine-looking face and yelled: "Surprise!"

20. *Remembering Secrets*

Life is funny — I mean to say, life is *odd* at times.
Here I am sitting in a car in New Mexico listening to my
girlfriend talking on her cell to my old girlfriend, who is
talking somewhere in California. And my mind wanders.
It does that sometimes, back to the hazy days of the past.
To that old girlfriend who was young then, as we all were.
And Africa – the ancient sage.

Sitting here, I'm remembering that old saw: *life is
something that happens to you while you are making other
plans.* It is so true, which I learned in Africa – the primeval
teacher – the Motherland. Long ago and in the fog of
memory Africa and that longhaired girl come back, as does
that crimson night.

She was tall, blond and white, so she stood out in
the streets of the African capital. But she stood out
everywhere we went. She was the kind of woman that
stopped men in their tracks. Later, after staring too long,
these men would send sheepish looks at their wives or
girlfriends to see if they had been caught.

Surprisingly she wanted to go with me, on that long-
vanished, rickety, old narrow-gauge train. An upcountry
adventure. A lark. In an adjoining sleeper, the connecting
door allowing a moment in time. A chance to learn about
life. At the time, in that swaying train car, I thought those

lessons would all be good. I was planning my life, fool that I was. Planning on simplicity. There was another plan in the works, the obscure contrivance of the Stranger.

At first it was a dream. We floated through those African days, traveling north, away from the sea, like children. Juveniles in love, blinded by the moment, the veil of youth hiding the veracity that not all serendipity is to be sought. Happenstance can be a cruel teacher. A dark, heartless fortuity was riding that train through the African night, an Unwelcome Passenger. The lessons of this Dusky Interloper were to brutally push me into another level of adulthood, an unwanted maturity to be sure. I remember that now, the lesson being my constant companion.

After days of rest in Kumasi and dreamlike nights of play, we resumed our journey upcountry, this time by mammy wagon, which is an open-air truck into which wooden benches had been arranged. It was packed with people, chickens, goats, bundles of goods tied with twine and more smells than the mind can imagine or the senses easily tolerate. Like the twine on the bundles, oppressive heat was the glue that held all together, the hustle and bustle of the Africans being unified by the all-encompassing jungle swelter.

Upcountry the temperature rose, but the humidity fell. But the sticky jungle glue was replaced by a new and ubiquitous binder – grime. As we journeyed along the red dirt tracks, cutting this way and that through the wide expanses of savanna trees and tall, stately termite mounds, each passenger acquired a thick coating of red dust. Our eyes, ears and nostrils became clogged with tawny soot so that, eventually we had to tie bandanas over our faces, bumping and jostling along on the hard wooden seats, gasping and choking from one village to another, bouncing as if in an oven of filth toward Bolga, that northern outpost that passed for a town.

Nowadays, sitting here in an air-conditioned car, the discomfort would prevent me from attempting such a journey, but then, in our salad days, we thought it was an exciting adventure, something out of pulp fiction. We imagined that we were playing – a frolic through some fantasy formed by the mind of Edgar Rice Burroughs or another such writer who had never been to Africa. We envisioned ourselves to be modern-day Victorian explorers, finding new, exciting people, places and events.

Now, sitting here listening to the two women talk, another part of my mind knows I couldn't make such a journey today. I wouldn't even attempt it. I know the Stranger. But then the young White Woman and I were puerile landlopers seeking all that was unique and exhilarative. Of course, as with many seekers, we got more than we bargained for. The Shadowy Passenger from the train had boarded our rickety mammy wagon, hunkered down as Fate is want to do, blending into the sweating humanity, braying sheep and cackle of chickens there in that crowded transport.

I really didn't *know* this White Girl, this modern-day Jane of Africa, just as I didn't *know* the Stranger. She and I became lovers who only knew the shimmering surface of our dreams. We had not yet delved deeper into the meaning of life or each other's hopes and fears. Or the past. And she harbored a dark secret, which burst forth in frightening force on that sweaty, grimy afternoon, somewhere in the red heat of the savanna. And it was only to be a foreshadowing of a deeper, darker enigma. Before that terrifying watershed, her face had been a picture of joy, a continuous smile on her unpainted lips, and a lilt to her voice, not unlike the misleading joy of a songbird's aria. My first hint that something was wrong came as I peered over the sweaty handkerchief covering my mouth and nose to see pain in her beautiful eyes, to become aware of tiny lines around the edges, a presage of decline, of the eventual decay that awaits all humankind. Death was scribing her face.

"What's wrong?" I shouted over the din of the motor, human conversation and animal clamor. "Are you in pain?" I saw a glimmer of fear pass over her dusty face, the small part that I could see above her soiled bandana.

Was it the fear of the secret? Was it the fear that I would eventually know that which she kept from me? These are questions I can now ask myself, sitting here in the car decades later, but at the time the unknown fear crept through the white heat of the African day and entered my body, lining my face with its furrows of unsought knowledge.

She made a slight nod, as if she didn't want to admit it to me or to herself. A frail attempt at a smile struggled through her eyes. Then it happened. The light went out of her and she slumped forward in obvious pain.

Sitting here today, I am not sure I can exactly recount the bafflement I felt, going from giddy togetherness to having an apparently ill girl on my hands. Hippies weren't supposed to get sick. And she was not only sick but also unconscious! I remember shouting for the driver to stop and I can still recollect the confusion that followed, everyone trying to help get the benumbed girl to the ground, a blanket here, a helping hand there. One traveler produced a water bottle and I gently held it to her lips. I remember feeling *mightily* relieved when she responded to the cold water, a slight flickering of the eyelids.

"Jennifer, what's wrong? What should I do?"

The beautiful eyelashes fluttering open, a moment of focus, then: "My pills..........."

"Pills? What...........?"

"My pocket. I have a ...." She seemed to slip away for a moment, to a place where she had to deal with the pain, a place of solitude where I could not go. Then: "My heart............ my heart pills."

In an instant I understood and the rest was procedural: pills, relief, some rest and back on the mammy wagon. But in that instant, my world changed and I was no longer in dreamland with a gaily-clad girl, but rather with a damaged one, a young woman with a past. A scarred past.

And now I know that I did not, at that moment of astonishment, know the full extent of the wound. I did not comprehend the history that would reveal itself in horrifying suddenness down that dusty road in the heart of the African bush. I remember thinking the problem could be solved with her pills. I was making plans, mentally configuring our future.

As Maddy and Jennifer talk on the phone, I recount in my mind the rest of the torturous journey to Bolga, or Bolgatanga as it is more fully known. Her wincing at every bump in the road. Her capacity to meet the pain head on, bravely, hunched in her seat in solitude. My relief when, several hours later, she had apparently recovered, the pills doing their job, her returning to normalcy, the strain going out of her shoulders. I remember her sitting upright and the return of her smile.

"I'm okay now." I hear these words today over the fuzzy airwaves of memory. I hear Maddy talking clearly now, but part of me also hears Jennifer's voice. Not the tiny one flickering out of Ann's cell phone, but the younger voice of long ago: "I'm okay now," as if the Dark Rider was no longer with us. As if the Visitor had only been teaching a momentary lesson.

It's hard to know how much of this I knew at the time. Perhaps my intellectualizing has clouded the moment, warped it with too much re-thinking. No doubt this has happened, as it always must, when we rework memories, but I do remember knowing at that long-ago moment that our lives had flowed together. I knew that they had been transfixed with a firmer adhesive – that a mature bond had been forged in the confusion of that African afternoon. The fire of lust was replaced, in an instant, by the temper of commitment, by a steely mingling of souls. Or so I thought at the time. Thoughts are such fleeting plans.

As I listen to two voices – Maddy next to me and Jennifer through the crackle of the tiny voice box in the cell phone – I remember arriving in Bolga. The taxi ride to the Black Star Hotel. I recall going up some newly swept cement stairs to the second floor and a big room with louvered windows on two sides. The bath was also big, with blue-based whitewashed walls. Life was returning to normal with a smattering of what fortunate people call civilization. Its other name is comfort and we were glad to have it.

We took long hot showers, the red dust turning to swirls of ochre down the drain, running off white bodies in Black Africa. The road grim trickled out of sight, a watery lie. We did not know that the Cimmerian had billeted nearby, in some unlit cave, in a dusky adjoining room, in a dark cavern. He had more lessons to teach.

I recall cheer coming with nightfall. We stood on the balcony overlooking the misty African town, fires sending up their wispy signals as if saying: "We are here, we have a hearth, we are alive." I can see the two youngsters watching, hand-in-hand, while the light receded and blacked out the smoky beacons of the town's fires, replacing them with faint flickers of firelight, a continuing whisper: "We are here, we have a hearth, we are alive." A quieter declaration in the hum of the night. A bulwark against the Stranger's arrival.

Maddy chuckles next to me, in an apparent moment of shared mirth, Jennifer on the other end chuckling most likely. And we laughed long ago, as we descended those fated stairs, swept so clean by the woman's broom, another breastwork against the darkness, their manufactured cleanliness yet another human plan.

We each carried a torch, or what we call a flashlight in the States. I went ahead, the brave Tarzan in our moment of fantasy. The electricity was out (again), something quite normal in this nascent African nation, its light less reliable than the fires burning beyond the cement walls of the Black Star Hotel. I shined my torchlight ahead – its yellow tunnel showing each pitted step as we went down into the coolness of the watered patio, with puddles lingering from the rain that fell while we were in our room. A husky muggy cloak hung over the courtyard, like a shroud.

I remember enjoying the sultry night, however. We were freshly showered, relieved of the journey's grime, trying to forget the little hitch her heart had introduced to our African dream. We ordered two large-bottled Star beers, and then two more. We were giddy and laughed rudely as the waiter took our order, so focused on each other that he almost melted into the dark night. We talked of things light, of the trivia of life – the mortar of relationship. We couldn't see the Unwelcome Teacher at the next table, nor hear his gurgling chuckles, our laughter and giddiness shielding us from knowledge. We were exhilarated by this respite from the day's travail. It was not to last.

I think I was sipping my beer when she said: "What?!" I heard the fear in her voice again and as I set down my glass. My mind was trying to organize itself around the heart trouble and what I needed to do if this was a new bout with her cardiac difficulties. But it was not a heart problem this time, though one could call it a variant of that genre, stretching the metaphor. Whatever we are going to call it (through the foggy labyrinth of time) it hit like a bomb, upsetting the manufactured sparkle of the candle-lighted eventide.

I remember that she called me by my African name – Salia. The fear from the mammy wagon had returned to her voice.

"Salia! Shine your torch over here!"

As I fumbled to find my light she stood up. As she did so, my eye caught the crimson glimmer of tragedy. A gory sheen in the candlelight of our table, which was feebly struggling against the darkness of the night. I finally managed to find the torch's button and flick it to on. I directed the beam at Jennifer, now standing with her hands dripping with blood, held out to her sides in an expression of horror, her head bent down in disbelief, her long blond hair tinged with her womb's blood. The torchlight caught a glistening scarlet reflection, ominous in its dominion, powerful against the opaque night, an abstract panel of scarlet flickering in the black night.

"My God!"

"Salia?" A questioning dread smothered her voice. It was tight and wound up in terror.

"My God! What is it?" My mind was reeling, not yet connected to my feckless utterances.

"Blood?" I stammered. "From where...........?"

"Salia?" she repeated helplessly. "I'm bleeding. The baby."

Then, in a terrible instant, I knew. My mind raced: *It couldn't be mine (not enough time). Whose? Why didn't she tell me? Was there someone else? Of course, you fool!* It is amazing how many irrelevant thoughts can cloud your mind when action is needed, paralyzing the body. I stood statue-like, the torchlight bouncing off the dread before me. There was a faint movement in the dark to my right, as if a Voyeur had repositioned himself to get a better view.

"Help me.........Salia, help me. I think I'm hemorrhaging. I'm bleeding."

My mind still froze the moment. *Blood? Hemorrhage? Baby? What?*

"Salia, help me." Someone was calling to me through the darkness, the dream fading off into the African night. Then she fell forward crashing into the table, the caliginous blood of her dress smothering the lighted candle. The darkness rushed in. I felt as if I was drowning, but the sound of her fall shook me to action.

The rest was functional. I picked her up and we staggered through the murky patio to the stairs. I got her to the room. I remember that she wanted to be alone. In the bathroom – the room where the walls would show that stain of her past. She was locked inside for what seemed an eternity. Alone in her blood, with her baby. Someone's baby. I was alone too, out there waiting, a new kind of isolation, a separate desperation.

I remember walking outside for a breath of fresh air, trying desperately to comprehend what was happening, to escape the stifle of the dingy hotel room. I left the door ajar. There was a balcony just outside, grimy with algae, white stucco spotted black. To the right were the stairs. I remember walking dreamlike to the top and sitting down. Sitting here in the car listening to Maddy and Jennifer talk, what I remember most is the blood on the stairs.

21. *Silence and Sex*

Henry Slicer hung out in the fishing village because it was a great tourist spot, with a great view of the cliffs and a beach to die for. But he also was in residence every summer because the village attracted lots of beautiful girls (and some not so beautiful) from all parts of Europe, especially from the north with its blond haired Nordic types. He especially liked them because they had a freedom about themselves that often led them to lollygag about the beach *sans* bikini tops.

The local men loved this, but the fishwives, who ran most of the affairs on land (they let the men have the open sea) did not take kindly to topless girls, especially since lots of these village women had more hair on their faces than between their legs. Henry found them shrewish and unattractive.

But he wasn't there for the local women, who tended to be in a constant state of nervousness, frenetic in their pursuit of money, houses and the goods to fill them. It was what they did, what they passed on to their daughters – a lustful acquisitiveness. Unlike the young tourist girls who radiated fun and freedom, these local ladies were slaves to their property. It owned them, riveting them into the village, much as the graves on the hill above the village cemented in the dead.

Henry's routine was to sleep till noon, arise, eat a hearty breakfast and hang out on the beach, sometimes playing Frisbee with the tourists. At times he took walks or photographed local scenes, but this was fill. It passed the time until five o'clock rolled around and Henry headed for the *taberna*, a local bar for fishermen (no women allowed).

Henry liked the atmosphere, where black-clad sailors lounged about drinking from jugs while prone on gritty wooden benches. The joint was thick with cigarette smoke, with most every patron draping a handmade fag from one side of his lips, while pouring ample amounts of red wine down the other side. This sometimes resulted in their cigarettes demonstrating a purple base, the saturation and color increasing the more they drank. Eventually, most of them passed out on their benches, snoring and farting – adding to the chauvenistic "charm" of the *taberna*.

But the macho charisma of the tavern was secondary to the fact that they served Portuguese brandy for ten cents a shot. For thirty or forty cents Henry could climb quickly upon an alcoholic cloud, prepared for the night's hunt.

Once fortified with Portugal's equivalent of rotgut brandy, Henry would venture out into the evening, strolling through the outdoor cafes looking for a girl eating alone. A native English-speaker, he also could speak the local language, Spanish and French, which enabled him to communicate with almost any young and tender thing who had not yet hooked up with a man, which – after all – was the goal of many of the single girls who frequented the picturesque seaside resort.

On one very bizarre occasion, however, Henry's linguistic prowess failed him. He had been promenading through the village as usual when he spotted a rather plain, but cute girl who was eating alone in the *Restaurante do Mar's* outdoor plaza, which had a great view of the beach, the famous cliff and passersby as they sauntered along the boardwalk.

Henry signaled to the waiter and told him that he wanted a table next to the girl. He slipped the server fifty escudos and took his seat. He began his routine. He would first catch her eye and smile, perhaps raising his wine glass in a salute. Then he would lean over and speak to her in the language he thought would most likely go along with her physique and looks. The blonds got English, while the darker skinned or dark haired ones got Spanish. Few Portuguese girls would be dining in such an expensive restaurant. If these languages didn't do the trick, he tried his French, which according to the high standards of *L'Académie Française de Langue* was only passable. Henry used it only as a last resort, since the French girls could be snooty anyway.

On this particular night, he caught the girl's eye, smiled and raised his white wine in the air, nodding pleasantly. She responded with a broad smile and nodded too, with an appealing blush spreading across her alabaster face. He noticed that she had many small moles, which given her milky skin gave her the appearance of having been splattered with dark paint.

Henry employed his next standard procedure – the moved his right hand from horizontal to vertical quickly, pointing it in the direction of her table, at the same tilting his head in the same direction as the uplifted palm.

The girl's cheeks became rosier, but she nodded in agreement. Henry moved quickly into the chair next to her and said hello in English. The girl grinned but shook her head. She didn't have a Mediterranean look about her, so he went directly to French, but again she shook him off. Spanish and Portuguese also elicited similar responses with nervous giggles.

Henry was out of languages, so he smiled and shrugged, raising both palms to the darkening sky, at the same time raising his eyebrows as he tilted his head to the side. This seemed to be a universal language because the girl laughed lightly and repeated his gesture.

For the rest of the night they got by non-verbally, which apparently worked because after dinner they strolled arm-in-arm down the walkway along the beach. This lasted till about ten in the evening when the girl made the "sleep" gesture, putting both hands together beside her head and tilting it to indicate that she was tired and wished to return to her room.

Henry made a motion that said: "show me the way" and she pulled him down a cobblestone alleyway, winding through the quaint houses till they arrived at a hostel. They stood awkwardly at the base of a long flight of wooden stairs that led up to a balcony and four doors.

Without language Henry was unsure of himself. *Should I just kiss her goodnight? How can I ask her if I can come up?* Just when Henry was thinking that the night was a bust, she gave his arm a tug and started up the creaky staircase.

Henry learned three things that night. She was renting the room behind door number one; the tiny moles covered her *entire* body; and great sex can follow an evening of silence.

22. *The Color of Death*

Josh knew that he was dying. He didn't know much else, except that the hospital machines kept beeping and tubes ran in and out of his body creating a dizzying network, which he thought of as the material manifestation of the drug fog in his brain.

The bad side of the drugs the doctors had given him was that he couldn't catch up with his mind at times. It kept coming and going and sometimes he was six years old and sometimes he was a lonely old man in a hospital bed, with lots of unpredictable stops in between. At the moment he was trying to figure out whether dying was a journey into blackness or whether he was going to encounter some bright light and be ushered into a sparkling kingdom.

In his hazy mental state he was actually trying to figure out *why* he was trying to figure out the nature of black and white. *Am I going crazy? Why does this seem important? After all I'm dying!*

His mind flitted back over his life, stopping off at certain points where – for some strange reason – he had encountered black people. Since he was a skinny white kid from a country town in the West with more cows than people, he hadn't known any black people while growing up.

Well, there *was* Shine. He was the only black man in town and his name revealed his occupation. Josh didn't know what a double entendre was when he was a kid, but he vaguely understood that Shine had two meanings.

Josh actually only saw Shine from a distance and never talked with him. Josh never needed his shoes polished, but apparently the farmers and ranchers did, in that long lost time that preceded Nike and all the other tennis shoes that have since flooded the world.

Daily Josh passed by Shine's stand, which was situated on Market Street, near the Five & Dime where Josh worked as a stock boy.

Laying in the world of tubes and bleeping machines, Josh's mind remembered that he made seven dollars a week and was paid with a little envelope that had dollar bills and some change in it.

I wish I would have stopped and talked with Shine, the dying man thought.

Josh's mind seemed to have a mind of its own and was jumping around thinking about all sorts of unrelated things. It was disconcerting – more than dying even. He wanted to know about death a hell of lot more than he wanted to be lying in a starched-sheet bed attached to a techno-whirl of flashing lights and buzzers.

Shine popped up in his mind again, maybe because the jet-black man had died and Josh was thinking about death – and about black and white.

Why black and white?

It was strange because when Shine died, almost everyone in town went to the funeral. Josh thought about this for a while and then remembered the old white wino who died in their orchard house. He wasn't a white wino in that he only drank white wine. Not that. He would drink any kind of wine, even the pink sweet stuff. If they had produced a chartreuse wine, the white wino would have guzzled it down. No, he was a white wino because he wasn't black like Shine. But he died like Shine, the difference being that no one went to his funeral.

Well, that wasn't entirely true, thought Josh's coming and going mind. The white wino's drinking buddy who found him lifeless in bed went to the funeral. His wino friend had found him dead but warm. That's why his buddy didn't know he was dead for a week after he died. He and his drinking friend shared Josh's dad's orchard house, a small place with a pot-bellied stove. The wino's bed was by the stove and his buddy kept checking his feet to see if he was alive and since they were warm each time, he assumed the white wino was still in the land of the living.

The buddy must have been into the wine bottle pretty heavy because the white wino hadn't said anything or moved for over a week. But maybe that was normal for winos, drinking away their loneliness in the orchard house. Wine and hospital drugs do strange things to the mind.

Josh thought it funny that the wino was white in a white world and Shine was a lone black man in a white world and no one went to the white wino's funeral, except the other wino, who was also white. *What a strange thing to be contemplating when I am on death's door.*

Josh's mind thought about that for a while and then a nurse came in and injected something into one of the tubes leading into his arm and he was off on another buzz in la-la land. After swirling around in drugville for who knows how long Josh concluded that Shine must have been a nice man because lots of people went to his funeral. White people, for they were the only kind in that dead-end town, except the Mexicans, who were kind of on the sidelines in those days. Probably still.

The burying of the town's only black man must have been an event. Josh had missed it, his mind remembered, because he was putting bicycles together in the basement of the Five and Dime at the time. But Josh's mind remembered wondering what color a black corpse is after a couple of weeks. Or any corpse, black or any other color. You think about things like that putting together one bicycle after another.

In the hospital bed, Josh's mind went about on its dizzying journey for a while longer and then the drug fog cleared a bit. Then the black and white thing popped up again. For some reason his mind wanted to think about black and white. *Why black and white?*

Josh thought long and hard about this and came to a conclusion, albeit a tentative one (he couldn't be too sure about too much at this point): *I must be thinking about black and white because I'm white and I lived with black people.*

Black people. Now there's a gloss. Which black people? Josh disappeared for a while, to where he didn't know, but he came back and was still caught up with this obsession with black and white. He thought about all the black people he had known after he left that small town in the West. He remembered the black kid in the army at Fort Sam in Texas. Josh couldn't remember his name but he remembered that the kid couldn't go to the movies with him, in town. The movie house was downtown, by the river, by the Alamo. Josh couldn't remember the kid's name, but he remembered that he was black and blacks had a problem with movie houses, apparently, or the other way around really.

Josh remembered being angry that his friend couldn't use his weekend pass to go with him to the movies, but he couldn't remember if he went alone or stayed with his friend. He hoped he had stayed in the barracks, his contribution to the protests that were going on in those days. Streets, avenues and boulevards hadn't been named after Martin Luther King yet, certainly none near the Alamo. Black people and white people were being killed then over something called civil rights. Josh's mind remembered that it was in the newsreels.

There must have been black funerals and white funerals. Shine and the wino.

Why the hell am I thinking about black people when I'm dying?

Josh's mind thought it was strange to be thinking about so many things that didn't seem to be connected to his present dilemma. His mind struggled to make some connection, like minds will do. Black, white, death, clouds, heaven, the halo around Jesus' head – they all swirled in a drug haze and Josh disappeared again.

When he came back he didn't know where he had gone or how long he had gone there, or even if he went anywhere at all. But when he came back from wherever he had been, he was still chewing over black people and white people.

Josh gripped the side of the hospital bed – hard. He had to get a handle on this. He thought for a long time, till his hands began to hurt and he let go of the bed rails.

When he relaxed, his mind decided that it was because he had lived in Africa.

And then there was the fact that I lived with a black woman.

Actually two black women, but one was an American and the other was in Africa. *Black and white.*

Black and white!

That must be it. That must be what?

He was off on a drug slide again and lost any chance of figuring out what it was.

When he got a grip again, not on the bed rails but on his mind, which hadn't been behaving too well since coming to the hospital, Josh thought of Oreo cookies. Somewhere in college he had read a book or an article about blacks who were called Oreo cookies because they were Uncle Tom's – black on the outside and white on the inside. He thought that must be connected to *Uncle Tom's Cabin*, but he had never read the book.

Oreo cookies. Black on the outside and white on the inside. Were there people who were black all the way through? Where does black begin? Oh yeah, the one-drop rule. How long ago did they drop that rule? Did they drop it? Am I white all the way through? What color will I be when I'm dead? Is this what people think about when they're dying? Funny. Odd, rather.

Then Josh laughed in spite of a mouth full of respirator. He did so because he had an image of himself as an anti-cookie. He thought the notion clever: *I am a reverse Oreo cookie – white on the outside and black on the inside. Or I tried to be. In Africa. And in America. It was easier in Africa. But I'm dying in America.*

His thoughts were straying again and he went on another journey for a while. To nowhere, but he came back.

In the hospital bed, Josh thought of his village in Africa. He called it *his* village because he had lived there, many times over the years. The villagers were *his* people, even though he was white and they were black. It had been easy there, or easier anyway.

Easier than what?

Josh was gripping the bed again, trying to think.

What does my mind mean? What was easier in Africa?

Then he knew. Black and white had been easier. It had been comfortable to be a little black there, even though he was white. When he lived with Latisha in the states it had not been so easy.

What does being a "little" black mean? His mind struggled to get a handle on the fuzziness of this idea. *If there are black people and white people, there has to be a point that separates them, black from white. Otherwise*

there would be a bunch of gray people in the middle.
Weird.

Josh's mind went in and out, back and forth, disappeared and returned and then it knew: in America he was forced to be The Man all the time, even at black parties. Maybe especially at black parties. Even though he tried to be a reverse Oreo cookie (he even learned to play spades and dominoes the "black" way), it had been difficult in the states because it was harder to overcome the history of the country – slavery, racism – all the bullshit. He was always seen as the enemy, but in the village he had an African name, an identity beyond being white. There he had obligations and privileges that were unconnected to whiteness or blackness. He had been considered to be family. In Africa he wasn't The Man.

In the village he could be the only white person many of the villagers had ever seen and still they had accepted him, taken him into their world.

While Josh was thinking about this and the contrast of Africa with the world African-Americans inhabit, he suddenly understood Shine. Just as Josh had been a solitary white man in the isolated African village; Shine had been a lone black man in a Western cow town. Josh was sad thinking of this. He was dying in the wrong place.

I should have died in Africa where people would have come to my funeral. Those black people were never alone in life, always talking, joking, visiting. And the funerals were humungous. Twelve-day funerals. Who ever heard of such a thing in America? African funerals were about life really. Lots of people, music, dancing – even girl-chasing. I liked black in Africa.

Suddenly in his loneliness and isolation, Josh thought he knew the color of death, but he had no one to talk to because the respirator made it difficult to call out to the nurses, the black and white strangers down the hall.

23. *The Helper*

Fran and I had been discussing how Wolf Kahn gets away with a lot in his abstraction of the landscape simply because he *is* Wolf Kahn, when the telephone rang. It was Jim Barnes, who was arriving for the oil painting workshop. He was flying in from Chicago and driving to our studio from Albuquerque.

"He's invited us to dinner," announced Fran. As an afterthought, she added: "You know that he's an avid vegetarian, don't you?"

"Yes dear," I replied. "Remember we were with him in Guatemala and he always prepared his own food. Wouldn't eat out in the restaurants, as I recall."

"That's him. Small guy with near zero body fat, I would say."

"Well, I'm gonna have a porterhouse steak, my dear," I said maliciously.

"Now now, don't be that way. Not everybody's a carnivore like you."

"Hun, I've been a vegetarian at times. In India, for example, I never eat meat 'cuz they break up the damn bones in the chicken and pork. And you can't get beef there, for obvious reasons. But the bone splinters can be damn dangerous, so I just stick to the vegy dishes there."

"Well, that's a different kettle of fish, isn't it?" she countered.

"Bad metaphor," I spat back.

"You know what I mean, honey. He is an *avowed* vegetarian. He eats the way he does out of commitment. He doesn't go somewhere, eat vegetarian and then go somewhere else and take up meat again. With Jim it's a way of life."

It went on like that, till we finally got back to Wolf Kahn and the infinite interpretations one can make about any style of art.

That took us up to dinnertime. We wound up at a local restaurant – Jim, Fran, two women who had flown in for the workshop and myself. When Jim excused himself to go "wash up," we naturally discussed his peculiarity and, in turn, each of us recounted a story or two about someone we knew who was "that way."

About the time that my turn came up, Jim returned from the bathroom, sat down and began to peruse the menu. I turned to him and explained that we were each recounting stories about vegetarianism and that my daughter had been a vegetarian once, until that is, she passed by a hamburger joint and the smell took her down the path to sin.

My story got mild chuckles and, being pleased with myself I took another sip of my Merlot.

Mary ordered first. She asked for a bowl of clam chowder and a Caesar salad.

A safe selection, I thought.

The next gal, Sally, got the trout. Fran wanted the prawns and when my turn came around I proudly announced that I was going to have the biggest steak in the restaurant – the twenty-eight ounce porterhouse. I think I must have had a smug look on my face.

And then the waitress looked at Jim. He smiled at her and said quietly: " I will have the hamburger with French fries, of course."

It seemed to me that everyone in the restaurant fell silent at once – just for a split second. Of course, this was not the case but at our table there certainly was the distinct sound of breath sucking and jaws dropping.

I hung my head. My big mouth and I had done it again. I had led another fellow down the path of gastronomic sin. My story about my daughter's fall from grace had made me a hamburger helper.

24. The Priest Who Loved the Jewess

In the sixteenth century, Venice was a squalid, but prestigious, city, with its many islands, canals and bridges. Jews flocked there, many fleeing the pogroms of 1492 in Spain. Spaniards at heart, they came to Venice to establish a new life and find a modicum of freedom. They were to find that they had exchanged one form of discrimination for another.

But there was another Spaniard in the city of water. He was a Priest, sent there as the Pope's ambassador to Serenissima, which was the Latin name for the city, meaning "the most serene one." His name was Father Diego Hurtado de Mendoza.

As was the custom with many men of the cloth in the Middle Ages and beyond, Priests, Bishops and Popes included, Diego had a wife and children back in Vitoria, a large city in Northern Spain. Nevertheless, when traveling for the Church he was not unfamiliar with the inside of the local bordellos, of which there were many in Venice.

But frivolity aside, Mendoza's mission in Venice was an important one as defined by Pope Julius II, known as one of the most aggressive of all Popes, hence his nickname – *il papa terribile.* Diego had been called initially to the initial convocation of the Fifth Lateran Council (1512), though as a mere Priest, he was not an official member of the Council. Rather, Pope Julius had wanted him there to meet with various Bishops, who gave him instructions as to his mission with the rulers in Serenissima, the Mantua family. The Holy Father was interested to know if the Mantuas were in collusion with France, with which the Papacy was at odds at this moment in Medieval history.

The problem, as the Bishops outlined it, was that the Bishop of Venice was a Frenchman, Bishop Jeanne-Pierre Beaufort and he was chummy with the Mantua family. Was a plot against the Papacy in play? Were Beaufort and the ruling family trying to push Rome out of Venice to the benefit of France? In other words, Mendoza was sent to Venice to spy on the Bishop and those in power in Serenissima. Much great wealth was at stake.

After meeting with the Bishop it was clear to Fr. Mendoza that he was not welcome in Venice, but the Bishop seemed resigned to the fact that the Pope had sent the Priest and he must appear to obey Rome's wishes. Beaufort played the gracious host, wining and dining Mendoza. He also invited him to a lavish dinner party thrown by the Mantuas, at which the newcomer was introduced to the Serenissima élite.

It was at this party that the Priest's life would change forever. It happened while he was in a particularly boring conversation with one of the Mantua daughters.

Over her shoulder he saw a serving girl enter the room, a tray of hor'douves in her hands.

There are moments in life that one cannot explain. They are instances at which time stops and the normal rules governing daily life fall away. A zone of concentration emerges, perhaps like that experienced by an artist or a musician, when the world disappears and he is able to focus on one thing and one thing only.

To the Priest, it was the girl. She was beautiful, but not dazzlingly so. In fact, the world would define the Mantua girl in front of him as more beautiful, but there was something about the way she moved, an aura that hovered over her. He imagined that she left a trail of loveliness and harmony behind her as she moved through the opulent party, offering snacks to the rulers and their privileged guests. To Mendoza, she lit up the room.

"Father. Is anything wrong?" asked the Mantua daughter.

"Sorry? Oh, no. Sorry. I was just ... I was just thinking about something that was said at Mass this morning."

"Oh, you are so lucky Father. To live the Lord's work on a daily basis, to go to Mass every morning. It must be nice not to have to deal with the humdrum details of life we common people have to face every day."

Mendoza knew that he was being buttered up and went along with the banter, glancing from time to time at the striking servant girl, who finally dispensed all her delicacies and exited by a side door.

The rest of the evening was taken up with small talk and Mendoza was unable to focus on his mission – to find out if Beaufort was up to anything sinister. He seemed to be frozen by the experience of seeing the servant girl. He was a man of the world, in the sense that men in Medieval times, even Priests, Bishops and Popes, had mistresses; but he had never been smitten by a woman before.

The Priest sleepwalked through the rest of the night and eventually found himself in his small room attached to the vestry. He took off his Priestly robes and laid them aside. He climbed into bed and shut his eyes – tight. He wanted to remember her, to recall every detail of the few minutes he had been in her presence. Her image haunted him and he could not sleep. He tossed and turned. He tried prayer, but that had never really helped him through the years. He was a secular Priest, having entered the Church because, as a younger son, he could not inherit the family's estate in Álava. But he suspected that God and the Devil were real and as he fell into a fitful sleep, he was sure the Devil had sent the servant girl into his life.

****

Pedro, the Priest's manservant, was surprised when he got up. The Father was already up and gone. It was unlike him, as he was normally a late sleeper, in effect having no employment that required him to be anywhere at a certain time. Pedro had always been amazed at such men. They were born into wealth and lived off of the Church, which lived off of poor people like Pedro and his family. When Mendoza drank his whole bottle of red wine with a hearty meal, peasants toiling in the fields had paid for it. This irked Pedro, who wasn't sure there was a God, but he knew there was a Devil and at times he suspected that the latter was running the Church in Rome.

As he went into the Father's room, he was struck by the fact that his normal habit, the one he wore on a daily basis, was still lying on the chair by his bed. Pedro opened the closet and found an empty hook. *He has taken his best garments. Where could he be going in such elegant garb in the morning?*

****

Father Diego Hurtado de Mendoza found the gondola dock he was seeking. He figured that she had to pass through this one to get to the Mantua residence, which was only accessible by water. The boatman was waiting in his gondola, smoking a pipe.

"*Buenos Dias,*" he said in Spanish.

The boatman looked up and replied, "*Et le bon matin à vous, Père.*"

Mendoza switched to French. "I wish that you assist me in a ... a venture."

"I am at your service, Father," came the lugubrious reply. The gondola owner deftly jumped up onto the dock. "How can I help you?"

"Is this the only station to go to the Mantua mansion?" Mendoza knew that it went there, as he had taken a gondola from here to go to the party, but he was not sure if there were other gondola stations nearby.

"*Vous avez raison.*"

"There are no other?"

"Non, *Père, seulement ceci l'un.*"

"The only one. Great." Mendoza hesitated. He was not exactly sure how to go about asking the man about a girl whose name he did not even know.

The boatman waited with a quizzical look on his face. "You are a friend of Monsieur Mantua?"

"Yes, yes, of course. Look here. Do the servants of the Mantuas pass through here?"

The man raised his palms to the sky and shrugged his shoulders: "How else, Father. They don't swim there," the boatman replied, laughing at his own joke.

"So you know them. I mean they come through here every day, do they not?"

"*Bien sûr.*"

"Good. Look, this is going to seem a strange request." Again, the Priest wavered. At times like this he felt out of place in his habit. How was he to phrase it exactly?

"Go ahead, sir. Anything." The gondola operator could smell money in the deal.

"When I was at a party at the Mantua house the other night I saw a girl, a servant girl. I don't know her name but I want to meet her." There it was. The man could think what he wanted.

The boatman smiled broadly. He immediately knew the girl in question. More than one man would like to meet her, of that he was sure. She had *it*, that special attractiveness without being overwhelmingly beautiful – raw sex appeal. "Yes, Father. I think I know the girl you mean."

"Do you know her name or where she lives?"

"No, I don't know her name. She goes to work in the mansion with the other servants. They are all Jews, so I assume they live in the Jewish Ghetto."

"Jews?" Mendoza was caught off guard.

"That's right. The Mantuas only employ Jews.

"Why for God's sake?"

"Well, I don't rightly know, but I have my suspicions."

"Oh. I see," replied Mendoza, wanting to move on. The background of anyone, the girl or the Mantuas, was of no importance to him.

"Have the servants come through here today?"

"*Oui monsieur. Ils sont au manoir maintenant.*"

"And what time to they generally return?"

"Well, it varies. Sometimes I am not here, but my son takes over. But I think it is usually around four o'clock. They have to be in the Ghetto by dark, you know."

Mendoza mulled over what he had learned. He must have been lost in thought for some time because the boatman finally said: "Is there some way I can help you, Father?"

"Oh…yes. Yes you can. Will you be bringing them back this afternoon?"

"Normally that is my son's shift, but if you like I can be here."

"No, I guess that is not necessary. I know what she looks like." The Priest reached into his tunic and produced a gold sovereign.

The gondola operator beamed. "God bless you, Father. God bless."

As he walked away, Mendoza said under his breath: "No. No, I don't think He will."

****

Father Mendoza was at the gondola stand a half-hour early. He noticed that the old operator was gone and a younger man was in the boat, doing repairs of some sort. After some time, as if it was a routine, the boatman put away his gear and began to pole the gondola in the direction of the Mantua residence.

After about forty-five minutes, he was seen poling toward the dock, his gondola full of people. As they neared the pier, Mendoza could see her and his heart began to flutter. He didn't like the feeling. He knew he was out of control, but there it was. He was smitten and he had to follow his fate.

The sun was setting low in the winter sky and the Priest hung back in the shadows. He watched as the servants stepped onto the dock, some going off immediately, and others hanging around talking. The girl seemed alone and began to walk in the direction of the Ghetto. Mendoza followed her at a respectable distance.

It was a walk of about ten minutes and it seemed that the gondola operator had told the truth. She arrived at the Ghetto gate and quickly went in. Apparently she was unaware that she had been followed. Over the course of the next few weeks, that would change.

****

He liked it when she did not go straight home, as he could not follow her beyond the gates of the Ghetto, certainly not in his priestly robes. On this day, she went to the market to buy vegetables. This gave him more time to observe her, to marvel at her feminine movement, at her grace.

She was at the vegetable vendor's stand and Mendoza positioned himself in front of a stall selling trinkets. He feigned interest in buying something and thought that she was unaware of him, as she had been during the many days he shadowed her after work. At times, when especially in need of seeing her, he would wait outside the Ghetto gates to follow her to the gondola.

Mendoza was just about to steal a glance at her when she was standing right in front of him. Startled, he stepped back.

"I believe you have been following me, Father. Is there something I can do for you? As you have followed me to the Jewish Quarter many times, I assume you know that I am not of your faith."

Mendoza blushed deeply and stammered something unintelligible.

The Jewess waited, holding her basket of turnips.

The Priest regained his composure and said: "I apologize miss. I did not realize that you knew. How long?"

"Weeks. A girl has a sixth sense about such things."

"I want to assure you that I mean no harm. It is just that … that…" Mendoza did not know how to phrase it.

The girl cut in: "Some weeks ago you were at the Mantua party, were you not?"

"You remember me?"

"You were the only Priest there, *Padre*, except for the Bishop, of course."

"Ah, yes. I forget about my appearance at times. I am so used to this garb by now. It seems normal."

"It is not normal for a Priest to be following a Jewess, especially one who is a mere servant girl, don't you think *Padre*?"

This is no normal girl. I am on the defensive already with this one. "Well, you seem to be a straightforward talker miss. So I will be honest with you. But not here, not like this. May I buy you a coffee?"

"*Por supuesto*. I have nothing else to do at the moment."

Father Mendoza guided the girl to a nearby café, which had tables facing the canal. They selected one with an umbrella and sat down. The waiter appeared immediately.

"*Due caffè per favore*," said Mendoza.

"Ah, you speak Italian. Should we speak in Italian?" the girl asked in Spanish, the language in which they had begun speaking.

"No, no. That was just for the waiter. I am Spanish, of course. Like yourself, I believe."

"My people came from there after the time of trouble."

"Yes and unfortunate period in our history."

"We are getting used to these … unfortunate periods, as you say. The first pogrom, at least the first one we remember, was a hundred years before Ferdinand and Isabella's expulsion order."

Mendoza raised his right hand to the sky. "But let's not talk of unpleasant things. I don't even know your name. I am Diego Hurtado de Mendoza."

The girl smiled. "Mine is Sophia."

"Well, I'm relieved. I thought it might be Maria."

"I am a Jew, not a Papist."

Mendoza laughed. "Of course, not all women in Spain are called Maria, just most of them."

The coffee arrived and they halted their conversation to prepare it, then Sophia abruptly asked: "Why are you here?"

Mendoza was confused. "You mean why am I following you?"

"No, we can get to that later. I mean why are you in Venice? You are a Priest, but you don't have a parish. Furthermore, you seem to have a lot of time on your hands to follow young girls about the city."

Mendoza was relieved to see that Sophia was smiling when she said this. "I have been ordered here by the Pope." He hoped that would satisfy her.

It did not. "To do what?"

"This is strange talk. Why would you want to know this, a beautiful young girl like yourself?"

Sophia persisted. "There is already a Bishop here, Jeanne-Pierre Beaufort. He is the Pope's man in Venice, is he not?"

"Of course. I am only here temporarily. Bishop Beaufort is the resident papal authority here. Why are we discussing this? I want to talk about you."

Sophia went on as if he hadn't spoken. "So if Beaufort is in charge and you don't have a flock here in Venice, why are you here?"

Mendoza took a sip of his coffee. "If you must know, I am here on a diplomatic mission." He hoped that would satisfy this feisty girl. *What could she know of these things?*

"That covers a wide range of possibilities," she replied, drinking her tepid coffee. She wasn't much of a coffee drinker. "Specifically, why Venice? What is your calling? You are a Priest aren't you, or is this some sort of disguise?"

Mendoza roared with laughter. When he calmed down he said: "Yes, it is a sort of disguise, but not as you mean."

"And how do you mean it?"

Mendoza thought for a moment. "It is complicated. You have to know my background."

"I know who the Mendozas are. They are a prominent family in Spain. They are rich."

"Ah, yes. My family is well-known."

"They run most of the banks in Spain, is that not true?"

"That is true."

"Why are you a Priest and not a banker?"

"Some of my brothers are not bankers. Some are Priests too."

"That does not answer my question," Sophia insisted.

"You have to know how it works in my family. There is only one brother who inherits. The oldest one. I am a junior son of my father. Each of us who is not in line to inherit must find an honorable occupation outside of banking."

"It is a strange tradition."

"It is indeed."

"So you are a Priest because you were not allowed to be a banker. But why are you in Venice?"

She is not going to let up. "I told you – diplomacy."

"You told me nothing."

Mendoza pushed his chair back in frustration. "Okay, if I tell you can we drop the subject? This is not what I want to talk about. Why do you want to know such things, anyway?"

"I did not follow you. You have been a shadow of mine since the party at the Mantuas. I want to know what you are up to."

"That has nothing to do with why I came to Venice."

Sophia leaned forward. "I think we both know why you followed me, why we are sitting here today. That is not the issue. I will ask you again, why is a Priest doing nothing in Venice but chasing innocent girls through the streets?

Women don't usually talk to me like this. What a tongue this one has. Mendoza fiddled with his coffee cup and saw that it was empty. "Would you like more coffee?" he asked for lack of anything better to say.

"I am not a big fan of coffee."

"Tea then?"

"If you insist."

"And a sweet?"

"*Si usted desea.*"

It took a few moments, but Mendoza finally caught the waiter's eye. When he came to the table, Mendoza ordered: "*Un tè, un caffè e due rotoli dolci.*"

"I still want to know why you are here."

"Good lord! You don't give up. It's politics. No concern of yours. Why are you asking such questions? I would have thought you would be concerned with the fact that I have been watching you, not political matters."

"I have told you that I know why you are shadowing me."

"Are you sure?"

"A girl knows."

Christ! I have never met a bold woman like this before. The waiter arrived with the new order and Mendoza quickly took a huge bite of his sweet and nearly choked.

Now it was Sophia's turn to chuckle. "I perplex you."

When he had finally cleared his throat, he replied: "That is patently obvious."

"Then maybe you won't haunt me anymore," Sophia said maliciously, but with a smile.

"I am not haunting anyone." Mendoza was clearly getting frustrated with this exasperating girl.

"It seems otherwise."

"You interest me, Sophia." It was the first time he had used her name.

"You also interest me, Father."

"Call me Diego."

"Not if you are wearing the Church's robes."

"They mean nothing."

"They do to people thrown out of their homes by Rome."

Diego knew the history of Spain's infamous Inquisition. In fact, one of his family members had been a Bishop responsible for many of the atrocities against the Jews. "That ancient history. This is now."

"And my people are here now because of what happened in 1492. Why are you here?"

"That again?"

"That again."

"Okay here it is: I was sent to the Lateran Council of Bishops to learn about the situation here in Venice."

"The situation?"

"With the Mantua family. They are very powerful and Rome is always interested in powerful people."

"You are here to spy on my employers."

Mendoza eyed the last piece of his sweet roll. "You would not make a good diplomat."

"I am not trying to be diplomatic."

"That is quite clear."

"Well, I *have* been effective in determining that you are a spy. Not only do you spy on defenseless young girls, but you also are spying on the Mantua family."

"Now you are just trying to make me mad."

"Partly."

"And you are enjoying yourself."

"Did you invite me here to suffer?"

"No, but you did."

"I didn't invite you."

Diego pushed his plate away. "Christ! Can we stop the fencing?"

"*Bien sûr*. As soon as you tell me why you are spying on the Mantuas."

"You speak French too?"

"*Je parle beaucoup de langues*. Now answer my question."

"It is complicated."

"We have time. The gates do not close till dark."

"What would happen if you were locked out of the Ghetto? Where would you go?"

"I will tell you all of these things once you have been candid with me. If we are to be friends, you must be honest about who you are and why you have shown up following me around town."

"You told me that you knew the answer to that."

"Now who is fencing with whom?"

They were both silent and sat listening to the almost inaudible swish of the gondolas passing by, a steady sound punctuated by an occasional splash of the boatman's pole in the canal. They could hear the conversations of those in the boats as they approached the café and then as they disappeared around the bend, out of sight and out of earshot.

"Alright, I will explain as best I can," began Diego. "Rome asked me to try to figure out if Venice would stay faithful to Papal interests or if the Mantuas were moving in another direction."

"Does the Pope see them as enemies?"

"That is what I am supposed to determine. He wants to know how friendly they are with the French."

"He fears the French wing of the Church?"

"They are apostates!"

"The Bishop is French."

Mendoza was stunned. This girl seemed to understand the situation in more depth than would a servant girl.

Attempting to sidestep her implication, Diego said: "Bishop Beaufort was appointed head of the Venice diocese by the Pope himself. He is loyal to Rome." Then he thought to ask: "Have you ever seen or heard anything at your work that would indicate otherwise?"

Sophia thought for a moment, pulling at a strand of dark brown hair. "We hear things at work."

"So he is not loyal to the Pope?"

"No, I didn't say that. In fact, I have always heard him defend Rome to *Señor* Mantua."

"What else do they talk about?"

"I am not going to help you with your spying, *Padre*."

"I am not a spy. I'm just interested."

"In any case, now I think we should talk about why you want to sleep with me."

"What?!" The astonished Spaniard leaped to his feet and knocked his chair over in the process. The waiter rushed to help him put it upright, but Diego was already bent over to fetch it.

"Let me, *Padre,*" said the server.

"No, no. It's alright." Diego righted the chair and turned back to deal with Sophia.

She was gone.

Diego glanced down the lane and saw her hurrying in the direction of the Ghetto. In haste, he started after her.

The waiter shouted: "*Signore*! Your bill!"

Mendoza looked back at the waiter, who had his hand out. He fumbled in his tunic and produced a coin and slapped it in the outstretched hand.

"*Grazie*," said Diego.

"*Grazie a lei*," replied the waiter.

When Diego turned she was gone. He hurried to the Ghetto gates. They were still open, but he could not enter. Not in his priestly habit.

"What a woman!" he said aloud.

"*Prego, non l'ho sentita*," said an old man with a long beard, who was passing through the gates at the time.

"Oh nothing, *Signore*. Talking to myself. I just had a frustrating day, that's all."

"*Oi vey*! Tell me about it," said the elder, who hurried into the Ghetto as the gates closed behind him for the night.

****

It felt strange to be wearing everyday clothes again, his priestly habit still in the closet, but it seemed even more bizarre to be standing in front of the Jewish Ghetto at dawn. It was cold and damp and Diego drew his cape around his neck against the foul Venice weather.

Soon, an old man dressed mostly in black and white arrived and opened the gates. Some people were waiting to go in, but most came out and hurried off to perform their daily tasks. Horse carts of goods came and went and an occasional buggy passed him by, the clip-clop of hooves on the cobblestones ringing in the crisp morning air.

No one seemed to pay any attention to Diego, who waited near a vendor who was selling chestnuts. He bought some of the roasted delicacy and slowly savored their rich, creamy taste as he waited for Sophia to appear.

When she did, he no longer tried to hide himself, as he had in weeks past. He walked up to her and asked: "Can I get you some chestnuts? They are delicious."

She did not seem especially surprised that he was waiting at the gates at such an early hour.

"Yes, I'm famished, but I must hurry to catch the gondola. If not, I will be late for work."

Mendoza bought more of chestnuts and they hurried together in the direction of the gondola station. He wasn't sure how to begin and bringing up her startling question of the previous day didn't seem appropriate at daybreak, especially as she was hastening off to work. Instead he said: "Can we have tea again after you are finished at your work?"

With a mouthful of nuts, she nodded.

"I hope you don't mind my showing up like this. I … I just wanted to see you. Yesterday's parting was …"

"Abrupt?" she mumbled through a half finished bite.

"Yes, abrupt."

When she had finished her snack, Sophia said: "I can be that way sometimes."

"I see."

"No, not yet you don't. I don't think I'm like most girls my age, even like most women. I've been told this, anyway."

"I would have to agree. You are not like any woman I have ever known."

"Too bold?"

Diego glanced at her face, which was partially hidden by the head-shawl she wore against the morning cold. He could see her well-formed lips. They held the hint of a coquettish smile.

Diego played the diplomat: "Just different."

They reached the dock and the other servants from the Mantua family's morning shift were already crowding into the gondola.

"I must run. Thank you for the snack and for escorting me this morning."

"It was much more pleasant than trailing behind you."

"See you this afternoon."

"I'll be here."

"Ciao."

"Andare bene."

****

This became a routine for the Spaniard and the Jewess. Mendoza would meet her each morning at the gates, escort her to the gondola and then reverse the process in the evening. In so doing, they became closer, though it took some time before the Priest would spend the night behind the Ghetto gates, only to emerge at dawn arm-in-arm with Sophia. Members of the Jewish community grew accustomed to the familiar couple, coming and going. They assumed that Mendoza was newly arrived Jew from Spain, as no one would have suspected that a *Goy* would enter the Ghetto at night, let alone a Priest.

It was, then, quite a shock when the stranger's body turned up floating in the canal that ran alongside the Ghetto. Residents of the Jewish quarter also found it somewhat odd that Sophia continued to go back and forth to work as if nothing had happened. She did not appear teary-eyed, miss work or exhibit any of the normal reactions to such a loss. Her lover was dead and she went on with her life as if he was still holding onto her arm, smiling and looking at her in adoration.

Then she disappeared. The Ghetto was abuzz with speculation. Most expected her body to turn up in the canal, but it never did. No one in the Ghetto ever saw the cute little servant girl again.

****

Bishop Jeanne-Pierre Beaufort met with his boss at Auvignon.

"I assume that since you are here, you have good news for me," said the Cardinal without so much as a greeting, cordial or otherwise. He was a dour man, given to political intrigue rather than spiritual matters.

"We were correct. He was a spy from the Vatican. The servant-girl confirmed it."

"He was trying to find out about our dealings with those ruling in Venice?"

"Without a doubt. He was reporting back to Rome on a regular basis, though his investigations slacked off considerably when our pretty little thing sidelined him."

"Why were the … more severe measures needed then?"

"Apparently he was about to visit Rome. We just couldn't have that. This girl let us know and we had to take action."

"Hadn't they grown close? How did you get her to go along with this?"

"I read my Bible."

"You what?"

"She went for the same thing that got Judas."

"And did she meet the same fate, I hope?"

"No Cardinal. The last time I heard she had purchased a rather splendid house near Marseilles and was in the process of finding servants to run it."

"Well, she is doing the right thing," the Cardinal said with a smirk on his crooked face, "servants can be useful."

25. *The Smart Feral Cat*

I'm a cat, ya see? A feral cat. That means I live in the wild and take my chances with foxes and bobcats and guys like that.

I used to live with humans, but they got to be too much. I mean *too* much! It can be dangerous to your health to be around these guys. Not the bobcats and foxes – the humans.

Lemme tell ya why I became a feral cat. It was my choice. I used to live in a nice big house with a not very smart guy and his not so smart wife. I had it pretty nice. These dull people had won a bundle of money in something called the Powerball and I was living the life of Riley. By that I mean these folks left food and water out for me and I could eat any time I wanted. I had a room that was almost my own, where they put a little wicker basket and a nice soft cushion for my bed. They even made a tiny sandbox for me. I didn't even hafta go outside to take a crap. Sweet.

Everything was going along fine and then they bought a huge flat screen television set with some of that Powerball money and put it in the room where I had my bed. In my room!

Well, that didn't make me real happy, having to share the room with a TV, but it was what I kept hearing on that idiot box that eventually drove me to live in the woods. No, it wasn't the big inanities that came over the air – not Afghanistan and Iraq – not the big craziness. It was three small stories that came on what these dreary people referred to as *Headline News*.

I called it the *Insanity Channel*. It had really beautiful but stupid announcers. They acted like robots and laughed at their own jokes. That didn't bother me so much – cats can be pretty forgiving, ya know – but what got me was the little stories at the end of each broadcast. These vapid announcers called them human-interest stories. I guess most tedious humans were interested in them. I wasn't, that's for sure. Call me opinionated, but I didn't like most of them. In fact, they scared the hell out of me.

After listening to a bunch of these stories, I decided human beings were dangerous to be around. This sweet thing of an announcer would tell the story, then she and the guy with the "just right" hair would titter and show their perfect teeth. They seemed to think their stories were interesting enough to laugh at, but these human-interest stories made my very fine hair stand on end.

Three stories in particular made me take to the wilds. The first came on right after they put the television in my room. Initially I found the set kinda interesting. I'm a curious sorta guy, ya see. Anyway this story was a real eye opener. It was about a bank robber, a real airhead. He waltzes into a bank, goes up to the teller and hands her a note. He had written: *Give me all the money in your till and I won't hurt you. I have a gun.*

Well, the gal does what the note says. She stuffs all the bills into the plastic sack this idiot so kindly supplied and he skidadles. Seems like he may have gotten away with the robbery, except he musta been as dumb as a load of rocks. Ya see, he had written the note on the back of his deposit slip and left it behind. The cops probably weren't much smarter than the robber, but they sure were smart enough to read his address on the slip and they were waiting for him when he got home that night. He showed up carrying a bottle of champagne. I guess the dummy was planning on celebrating.

Now that story made me sit up and take notice. I thought long and hard about being in close proximity to these human fellas.

But after a while I got used to the noise of the television set. If I didn't listen to the stories closely, it was even kind of comforting, like the tick-tock of a familiar clock or something. But every time the *Headline News* came on, I used that time to preen myself and listen in more closely. I thought I might learn something more about humans, which seemed important since these people were supposed to be taking care of me.

So then I hear the second story that gave me a fright. It went like this: a human guy finds a mouse in his home. It musta been in the autumn, 'cause this rocket scientist grabs the mouse by the tail, carts him outside and throws him into a pile of burning leaves. Now, this sadist was about to pay dearly for that mistake. The mouse's fur catches on fire, which made the mouse a little uneasy and he runs like hell, right back into the guy's house.

Well, ya can figure out what happened, can't ya? Right. The flaming mouse runs into the hole in the wall, sets the wall on fire and the Marquis de Sade's house burns to the ground.

After hearing that one, I started to work out an exit plan. I spent a lot of time looking out the window at the fields and woods. They were looking a lot better every time I had to listen to the *Insanity Channel*. I was getting the idea that humans were dangerous to be around.

Then came the *coup d'grace* – that's French for the final straw, ya know. Anyway, this is the yarn that feralized me. Ya see this gal in the TV story has a cat. A cat like me. A nice cat. She likes the cat apparently. She gave the cat a bed like mine, she fed the cat every day and she even had a little plastic box with that tan sprinkly stuff they call Kitty Litter in it. It seems she liked her cat very much. She liked her cat so much that one day she gave it a bath and after putting the poor thing through that ordeal, she stuffs her little kitty cat in the microwave to dry it off.

At the end of the story this beauty of an announcer with perfect teeth showed them off as – smilingly – she announced that they never could quite get the cat splatter off the inside of that microwave and the lady that liked cats so much had to pitch it in the garbage.

Now that's when I decided to take my chances with the bobcats and the foxes. They're dangerous, but they ain't *stupid* and dangerous.

26. *The Gin Visit*

We were in my Toyota Corolla, driving through the Nigerian rainforest, approaching the Niger River. That's where Ngozi's village was, her ancestral village where all her relatives lived. I was a bit apprehensive, driving through the sweltering day, wondering what I had got myself into. A White Man like me and a Nigerian girl like Ngozi going to meet her people.

Sitting here now, all these many years later, older and somewhat wiser about certain things – certainly about visiting Nigerian relatives – I remember the beauty of the forest, with its low-hanging branches, its jungle sounds, the leaves and fronds dripping with sweat. I remember entering the village by way of the river road, with the Niger's traffic – the fishermen and traders in their dugouts – polling and paddling through the day's work. Their black bodies glistened in the noonday sun, an ivory sheen on ebony bodies. This was the Africa of the tourist brochures, the closest one could come to the adventurous spirit of the Victorian explorers like Livingston or Stanley. This was the West Africa I had always envisaged, as a young lad reading the Tarzan books – dreaming of adventure.

I remember being in somewhat of a daze as we parked the Toyota in front of Ngozi's parents' place, a fairly modern cinder-block house with green louvered windows and a path leading through a well-manicured garden of brilliant flowers and greenery, what her father called his miniature jungle. He was a nice man and Ngozi's mother was also very agreeable, but they were both leery of me. Being with their daughter, as I was, unmarried and obviously sleeping with her, they had a right to be concerned.

But they were understanding, more so than I had expected. For example, they put us together in a single bedroom with a double bed and rather comfortable accouterments for Nigeria in the 1970s. Clearly, they had gone to some effort to make our stay comfortable. It was, as I recall, all very modern both in the accommodations, their house being middle-class by Nigerian standards and in their attitude toward me, as someone sexually-involved with their young daughter.

The rest of the family members and villagers were to prove to be of a different ilk.

I remember putting up our things, bathing, eating an evening meal and retiring to the room they had fixed for us. I remember a night of unbridled erotic bliss, there in her parents' house. Ngozi was never one to be inhibited in that way, not even in her natal village, surrounded by all her relatives and with, in the African sense, her ancestors looking on.

The next morning, as I recall, we had a brief breakfast after which I was informed that we had to make the rounds to visit her various relatives, the most prominent members of her extended family. By the time we arrived at the first place, a traditional forest hut made of mud walls and roofed with palm fronds, it was a couple of hours before noon. It was already hotter than Houston on its worst day. This was, after all, tropical Africa.

We went through the normal, rather lengthy, greetings – all smiles and light-headed giggling from all involved. Everyone was nervous, though I remember the man of the house being very gracious, giving me a seat of honor on a mud bench, while Ngozi and everyone else either sat on stools, some carved in the form of elephants, and others merely squatted on their haunches, African-style.

I remember this first visit most clearly, for reasons that will soon be obvious.

The man of the house, who was reported to be a local medicine man, sat on his elaborately-carved stool to my right, near the head of the bench, which I remember having had a funnel embedded in the dried mud. As I was nervously involved with the greetings, being in new surroundings and coping with cultural differences, I did not at first think much of the funnel or the significance of the mud bench.

When we were all seated, the man of the house, who it turned out was the most senior man in the village, a very respected elder, made a slight movement with his hand and a brightly-clad woman of some years came forward with a filthy encrusted bottle of some sort. With a little curtsy, she gave it to the elder.

Fondling the bottle in his hands, the man was beaming, his perfect white teeth gleaming against the duskiness of his face, like the grill on a 1953 Buick. He was evidently tickled about something.

All the greetings and conversation took place in a mind-boggling mish-mash of the King's English (slaughtered form), a local pidgin and their native tongue. Ngozi translated for me when necessary, which became more essential as the day proceeded, as will be clearer as you read on.

Since I was struggling to follow the complexities of the conversation and to be as gracious as I could be under the circumstances, I did not think about the bottle or the funnel or even why the mud bench was there. The significance of the three would soon reveal themselves.

The elder scooted his elephant stool a bit closer to me and raised the bottle for all to see. He smiled broadly and let off a string of local words that Ngozi did not translate for me, but which were obviously meant to explain the significance of the bottle to those in the tiny, dusky room. With another wave of his hand he signaled for a cloth, which a young bare-breasted girl brought with some dispatch and the elder began to wipe off the greenish grime that had obviously lived on the bottle for a number of years. He rubbed the bottle, much as a genie would rub a magic lantern, all the time grinning ear-to-ear.

In the hubbub of the dimly lit room, the label on the decanter emerged, becoming clearer with each swipe of the soiled cloth. It was an ancient bottle of Gilby's Gin, which had probably been in his possession since the Colonial Era.

Now I'll tell you up front: I am no gin drinker. I don't like the taste and it gives me a headache, more than other spirits, for example scotch, which I prefer in the single malt version when at all possible. In the swelter and intercultural confusion of that African hut, on that particular day, it was to be gin. Old Gilby's Gin.

Inching even closer to me, the elder held the booze for all to see, swinging it around in wide arcs for all to observe and solemnize. He was evidently proud of this gin bottle and he was going to play the moment for all its worth. Then, with his powerful cream-palmed hands, he had the top twisted off and was pouring me a water glass full. Where the glass came from I didn't see, but with magical swiftness, he had the glass full and was holding it out to me.

I remember thinking: "It's ten o'clock in the morning and this cat is giving me eight ounces of straight gin to drink."

"Take it," commanded Ngozi.

When I did, more glasses mysteriously appeared and gin was poured into them, though not as much as my brimful. When every adult in the room had a glass (some were drinking from gourds), the elder evidently rattled off some kind of toast, elevating his glass from time to time, which he held in his right hand, the gin bottle in the other. With his Cheshire cat grin, he looked like a kid at Christmas.

After what seemed an awfully long soliloquy, the rhapsodic elder came to an abrupt halt and tilted his glass toward the mud bench, a drop or two of gin falling into the mouth of the implanted funnel. Then, with his teeth flashing, even in the darkened room, he inclined his head toward me and then toward the hole in the bench. His eyes seemed to say: "Go ahead. Do it."

When I hesitated, trying to figure out exactly what was going on, Ngozi said: "He wants you to pour some gin to our ancestor."

"In the funnel?" I queried, stupidly, especially for an anthropologist, the vocation for which I was trained.

"In the funnel," she repeated. "It leads to the ancestor's mouth. He's buried under you, in the altar." She nodded toward the bench on which I was sitting.

I must have jumped because everyone in the room broke into guffaws, those not near the funnel pouring a smattering of gin onto the dirt floor and drinking up. I still had not poured my libation to the skeleton under me so Ngozi repeated her bidding: "Give our forefather a drink. You cannot imbibe before doing this. It is our custom."

I did as I was told, but being somewhat tense I managed to drain way too much gin down the funnel, which brought more guffaws from the crowd. I was the day's entertainment, it seemed.

"Drink up!" said the senior man in almost perfect BBC English. "Drink to the health of our forefather and his family, both those living and those dead." He raised his glass toward his lips, as if I needed a demonstration.

When I followed suit, more laughter filled the hut. The day's merriment had begun.

At first, I took just a sip, not liking the taste of gin, but not wanting to offend my well-disposed hosts. As the people in the room kibitzed and tittered, I slowly (very slowly) drained my glass. That was my first mistake of the day, unless it was getting out of bed in the first place. This was because, rather quickly, as if by some wizardry, my glass was again full.

"You like the gin? It's special," said my host.

"Uh, yes. It is very good," I lied.

Unfortunately, that day which stretched interminably forward through an alcoholic haze, was to put me off gin forever. The drinking bout was repeated again and again, at every hut we visited and Ngozi had a BIIIIIIG family. I think the sum total of her relatives matched number of brain cells I destroyed beside the lazy African river that day.

Somewhere I lost track of the relatives' names and their location in the familial network and, stumbling from hut to hut, from gin glass to gin glass, I don't remember much of anything beyond noon. But one thing did stand out when we returned to the first hut and I was again seated above the bones of the departed headman. I heard, or thought I heard, the senior man say: "Now my friend, we can begin to discuss the bridewealth you owe."

That was very expensive gin, to be sure.

27. The Other

Dear Mom and Dad:

I'm in a fix, so you're gittin' this letter. Here I've been given a direct order from the President Emperor. You folks at home know that it's a great honor, to be picked to lead a group of soldiers to kill the Other. You're my parents, so I guess I'd like your advice. What should I do? I've been instructed (you know – ordered) to kill the Other wherever and whenever my men find him, her or them.

But we haven't been able to *find* the Other. We've looked. Believe me, we jus' don't seem to be able to come up with anyone to kill. I have the *President Emperor's Handbook.* I've read it cover to cover, borin' as it is. Says the Other has to be sufficiently *different* from us so as to make 'im or her or them Sub-Human. I sent you folks a copy, so I guess you know the way we're supposed to be able to tell: different religion, different race, different ideas – whatever. You've read it. You know what I'm up against here. This is tough.

I even got my guys polishin' their bullets and grenades. Some of the especially-gung-ho guys have scratched little messages on them like: "Here's one for you Camel Jockey!" or some such thing. We spend hours cleaning our rifles and such. All spit and polish we are, but we don't have a single kill. Not a one! We can hardly hold our heads up in the mess hall. Lot of the other guys seem to find the Other easy-like. Sometimes I think they're more "other" than the Other. I dunno, it's confusin' – that's all I know.

The thing is – we can't seem to get past all the similarities – my squad that is. I know, and my men have been trained, that we should look for differences, first and foremost. We're even supposed to shoot first and ask questions later, that is if the guy or gal looks suspicious or dresses a little funny – you know. You folks have this type back home. We used to see a lot of them when we all took trips to the city – remember?

But back then, when I was a kid, we never got a chance to meet these people – to talk to them. We jus' assumed they were Other. The kids at school jus' called 'em gooks or spics – you know, like that. The N-word and stuff. But out here we pull somebody over and talk with 'em and try to find out if they're the Other and it's hard. It's hard to know if they're really Sub-Humans cuz – you understand, I'm sure – when you get to *know* them, after you've talked with 'em a bit, they seem too human. Hell, they got two arms, two legs and they're shakin' jus' like you and me. Jus' like we would if some foreigner stuck a rifle in our guts. Too human to kill. So we let 'em go.

Me and my guys are frustrated. And we get looks from the other guys in A-Company like we're the Other.

Go figure, jus' cuz we got no kills. Sure, I know my job's
to ferret out the Other and kill it. But it's not like it was
killin' squirrels as kids. You see a squirrel in a tree and it's
easy – blam! One dead Other. Over here it's more difficult.
Hell – they ain't even got trees or squirrels here! (ha-ha).
But we got lots of Raggies that look different – that we got.
But when ya really talk with 'em – well, it's hard cuz turns
out they got kids and hopes and dreams – all that stuff that
you folks back home have. You know what I mean?

  This killin' thing is harder than I thought. Take the
other day: we go out on patrol. Were locked and loaded.
We spot this kid, maybe ten years old, or so. He's playing
War and he's got a toy gun and everythin'. Made out of
wood and some wire and stuff. Looked real. He's dartin'
in and out of the mud houses, takin' aim. Playin' like he's
shootin', sayin' "blam" and "pow" and stuff like that.
Probably in his funny language. We cornered the little
bugger and scared the *you know what* out of him. If he
hadn't been wearing one of them dress-thingies they wear
over here – well, he would have done "it" in his pants.
That's for sure. (ha-ha).

  But we thought he might be the Other, dartin' round
like he was. Seemed like he was doin' Real War, not jus'
play war. Well, anyway we got 'im up 'gainst the wall and
he was jus' a kid. You know, young and real scared. His
war-game had turned bad on 'im. Real quick. I could see

he was scared, jus' like I was that time Billy Hunter pointed his pistol at me by the river. I could see it in his eyes. He felt like I felt back there lookin' at Billy's twenty-two. Turns out, he wasn't the Other. He was jus' like me back home – scared out of his gourd. We played with 'im a bit and then let 'im go. I don't know if he kept playin' War, but we told 'im to be careful. The real thing can kill ya. That's what we told him, kinda to keep 'im from getting' shot by accident. Some of the other guys in A-Company don't stop to talk to these kids. They jus' shoot. Figure he's an Other right up front. Little girl bought it the other day that way. With the dress-thing over here – you know – sometimes it's hard to tell.

So any advice you folks can give me would be helpful. I'm not doin' very well with this killin' thing. Or maybe I should write it "Killin' Thing" or even "KILLING THING." Who knows? It's big, that's for sure. Big over here. Lots of these people dyin' every day. I hope most of 'em are the Other, but sometimes I dunno. I jus' think maybe we make too many mistakes when we shoot real people thinkin' they're the Other. Then they're dead and you can't ask 'em, can't talk to 'em any more. But they look human, mostly, even when they're dead. You know, red blood runnin' out and all. You stay 'round the body long enough and they usually pee on the ground, relaxin' and all like the body does. Real humanlike. That's what the other guys in A-Company tell me, them braggin' 'bout their kills and all. Sometimes I think we make lots of mistakes.

Well, that's about it folks. I jus' wanted to get your take on all of this. Once you're over here in all this killin' it's hard to know. It's hard to figure out who is who. You know, sometimes after you've got to know these people they don't seem like the Other that the *President Emperor's Handbook* talks about. You know, mom and dad, they seem so Human. Or maybe I should write it "HUMAN" or somthin' like that. You know? Nuther thing: this ain't "ha-ha" over here.

Love,

Farley

28. Eyes of Death

As a kid I hunted for sport, which is a nice way of saying I enjoyed killing things. Part of it was the pleasure of making a good shot, with either a bow or a gun, but I have to admit that back then, in my Huckleberry Finn days, I continually roamed the countryside looking to kill birds, small mammals, feral cats, snakes – anything alive. During the appropriate hunting seasons I went after ducks, geese, pheasants, doves, quail and deer.

Ducks were my favorite because the farmers who let us hunt on their land had ponds and reservoirs that attracted migrating ducks. These had high levees that made it easy to simply, but quietly, walk up to the levee, crawl up, peek over, locate the ducks and sneak into a good position for a shot.

It was a real pleasure to jump up and see the frightened birds rise off the water, wings flapping furiously. I often got one or two on or near the water's surface and more in flight. Killing these ducks was even more pleasurable than my everyday killing ventures because, unlike feral cats and songbirds, we ate the ducks.

But as a country boy, I regularly shot birds and animals for the mere pleasure of killing. I remember that I once sneaked up on Carrie Lieddy's barn and sat there pumping one BB after another into a pigeon that was sitting atop the barn. For some reason the bird did not fly away and finally the accumulated shots brought the bird down at my feet bleeding and dead.

Apparently, the old lady who owned the place, Carrie Lieddy, had been watching my killing spree from her kitchen window. As I picked up the dripping bird she came out on the front porch and called me over.

"If you're gonna kill things, you gotta eat 'em." And she made me pick, gut and roast that pigeon over an open fire. Then she sat there till I ate it all. It was a lesson learned, though through the growing up years I broke the rule with skunks and varmints that were not palatable. I think I even eased off on the songbirds, which were too much trouble to pick.

All that was many years ago and I had not hunted much till I moved to Aspen Colorado and got the urge to go after Elk. Now there's good eating meat. Elk backstrap is superb fried in garlic butter. Hell – it's good done any way.

But again, even as an adult, it was less about eating than sport. I was after the thrill of the hunt, the shot and seeing my animal drop.

It was to be my last hunting trip and I am about to tell you why.

It was a crisp winter day when I headed up the trail, my backpack in place and my rifle at the ready. It meant something to me to use this specific rifle, which had been given to me by my brother Pat.

The ground was covered in deep snow, but hunters and horses had worn away most of the snow from the narrow, winding path that wound up the backside of Aspen Mountain. As I climbed I occasionally heard shots being fired in the distance, but I did not see anyone during my climb.

My trek took me up steep mountainsides to a series of plateaus, each of which was heavily wooded with a mixture of white Aspen trees and green pines. It was beautiful and the sun played peek-a-boo with white fluffy clouds, sending scurrying shadows over the landscape.

At each plateau I stopped to scan the landscape for elk. I saw none on the first three stops but then on my fourth try they were there – a whole herd slowing moving up the other side of wide snow-covered gorge. It was a long shot, but I knew that I could not traverse that ravine in deep snow fast enough to get to them and, anyway, traipsing through the snow would likely spook them.

I flipped off the safety and rested the thirty-ought-six on a jutting tree limb. I had drawn a cow tag, so I looked through the scope toward the end of the meandering herd for a fat cow. When I found one I slowly squeezed off a shot only to see the snow puff up to her right. She raised her head warily. In the round lens of my scope I could see her move her head around searching for danger, but she didn't bolt.

I quietly and slowly moved the bolt of the gun to eject the empty cartridge and it fell smoking into the whiteness below, melting its way down to the frozen earth. I zeroed in for a second shot. I put the crosshairs right on her shoulder and squeezed off another round. In a second or two I saw her hindquarters drop and she turned and began to try to run, but there was something wrong with one hind leg and she was having a hard time of it.

The big bulls at the head of the herd bolted and all the frightened animals began to run up the valley leaving the wounded cow behind. While the herd moved off to my right, for some reason the bleeding animal was moving up the steeper side of the mountain, directly away from me. I was going to shoot again, but then I saw her go down, a large brown spot in the blanket of snow on the opposite side of the canyon.

I took out my binoculars and watched her motionless body till I was convinced that she was dead, and then I started the laborious trek through the deep powder, first down, then up toward my prize.

To my surprise, when I drew near to her, she jumped to her feet and roared through the underbrush. I was caught unawares, with my rifle slung over my shoulder. Quickly I un-slung it and moved toward her sound in the bushes. I was totally unprepared for what happened next. I pushed through some willows, still unable to see her, but the sound had stopped. The willows were grabbing at my clothes making forward progress slow and tiring. I was breathing heavily, large frosty clouds of breath trailing behind me.

Once out of the dense willows, I came to a small clearing. I stopped and listened. It had begun to snow lightly, a fact that had escaped me as I pursued my prey. I remember thinking how beautiful the scene was. White flakes fell on the blued barrel of my gun, melting away quickly, as if dying.

I listened intently and picked up her labored breathing. She too was dying, I thought, melting away like the snowflakes. But it was not to be either beautiful or easy. I moved toward the sound, entered another thicket and pushed my way through to a large clearing.

She stood there, unsteadily facing the man who had shot her, as it turns out, not in the shoulder, where I had aimed; but in the hind leg, which I could see was turned wrong in the snow. Her three good legs were holding her up, but they were trembling and I thought she would go down any second.

I was still some distance from her, with few brushy trees between her and me, making a *coup de grâce* difficult.

I moved a little to my left, coming out into the clearing proper. Now there was nothing between us.

I raised the rifle to administer the deathblow, but as I sighted in on her forehead I was transfixed by her eyes, which were wide in my scope's lens. They seemed to be asking me "why?" "Why did you take this beautiful life from me?" I was stunned and lowered my rifle. We stood facing each other, a growing sadness darkening the glory of the wilderness.

Then she charged. With frightening speed she had almost covered the few yards separating killer from dying. I could see her wild eyes, which seemed all too human, as she bore down on me, as if coming in slow motion. No, *human* is not quite the right word. They were more than human. Her eyes expressed a sense of eternity, of the oneness of all life.

In an instant I understood and then I lost that flash of insight. For just a moment I grasped something important, but like the puffs of breath she and I made in the crispness of the morning, it evaporated and I knew that I would miss it for the rest of my life.

I don't remember raising my rifle and firing but I must have done so because I saw her forehead explode in a crimson burst, staining the pristine snowfall that had covered the hardened crust frozen from the night before.

Little craters of red dotted the clearing, giving it an unnatural aura.

She fell dead at my feet, the top of her head gone, but her eyes were still there, open and imploring. All the fury of the moment faded away, leaving only the sound of powdery flakes settling to the ground. I stood transfixed, watching as, slowly, the little red craters disappeared and the world became white again. Except for the dead body before me, the warm remnant of her life melting the snow as it lighted upon her.

As I stood there looking at the mist rise from her body, I imagined it to be soul-like and I threw down my gun. In the distance I could hear the killing shots, to my left, then coming from up the ravine to my right. Hunters at play.

I don't know how long I stood before her. I must have been in some kind of blind daze. When I came to see the world around me again, my rifle had disappeared in the new fallen snow. It did not matter. I would never need it again.

29. Sins and Suicide

Mark Hipple was very depressed after 911. All the media coverage (he watched way too much of it) made him tenser than ever before in his life. It made him sad. No, the truth is that he was depressed even before that catastrophe. *Al Quæda* had just pushed him over the edge. He had come to think that suicide was his only option. *"Easier than living!"* his night-terror mind screamed.

He was tired of the demons that visited his thoughts each night – each sleepless night. The restless, tired mind of a man at the end of his tether. *Rope – that was one way. A gun would be messy.* He was deathly afraid of heights. *How to go?* Suicide occupied his every waking moment, especially those that came to haunt him in the wee hours. As a young man, he didn't know that the dark night could speak, and in a deeply hurtful way.

An educated man, he knew of the larger epistemological questions, the most important being: Why is there *not* nothing. If the Big Bang came from a speck of matter smaller than a grain of sand, giving rise to the entire cosmos, as we know it, why did that speck exist in the first place? He had explored science, even string theory and found the answers there to be limited. Educated guesses were still guesses. So what if the universe (or was it the cosmos?) is made up of tiny vibrating loops of matter (or was it energy?). Why did they exist at all? Did some God make them, and if so, why?

And then, more terrestrially, why was there undeserved suffering? Why had there been so much injustice throughout history? Why did mountainsides slide down on whole villages in Latin America or Nepal, while people all over America were eating hamburgers and milkshakes or watching re-runs of *Seinfeld* on the idiot box? *Is God a trickster? A guffawing comedian?*

But these were the big demons and they actually were less troublesome than the earthly ones – those that stemmed from his life of mistakes and failures. Lost jobs, lost wives, lost kids. A load of lost opportunities. A derailed life, one barely acceptable in the light of day; but at night, sweating in bed, it was deplorable. He wanted out. Politicians who didn't care. Systems that didn't work. World poverty and a fourth of America's children going to bed each night hungry – in the richest country in the world. Even worse in the Third World. If not a Divine Clown, then God must be a sadist; at least that is how it seemed, heart-poundingly, at three a.m.

These were the dark thoughts that made suicide seem an easy, inviting form of escape from a misplaced life. There was only one problem: Mark had been raised a to be a devout Catholic and early on in his catechism classes he learned the difference between a venial sin and a mortal one. For the venial ones, you got a slap on the wrist, maybe a few weeks in Purgatory. Suicide was at the top of the list of mortal sins, right along with murder, and Mark Hipple had never killed anyone, even in Vietnam. And a mortal sin got you eternity in burning flames (Mark often thought watching re-runs of *The Brady Bunch* or *Leave It to Beaver* for eternity might be a worse fate).

Failure had dogged him all his life, starting with that big kid who took his lunch money the second day of the first grade. High school didn't get any better. Mark was smart enough to know that football was the pathway to power, prestige and pussy. He tried out for the team his freshman year. He weighed ninety-eight pounds and they used him as the football. He finally lettered in the sport – as a water boy.

He was even a failure in Vietnam, being given an early discharge on medical grounds. Nervous tremors or something like that on the Army's report. And he was nothing more than a G2 writer, a propagandist with a desk, for Christ's sake. He never even saw combat or the gore of the battlefield. At least those guys who saw their buddies blown to bits had an excuse, a valid reason to have "nervous tremors" – or worse. The most horrible thing that ever happened to him in the army was the time the air conditioning went out in Saigon. *I was just a failure.*

He read somewhere on the internet that gassing oneself was a painless way to go, but Mark had almost choked to death on a piece of bratwurst once and was saved only by a doctor who was eating in the same restaurant. He reasoned that gas might give him a sense of choking to death and he certainly didn't want that again. *I wanted a painless life and didn't get it. Now I want a painless death. I deserve that, don't I?*

Finally, after hours on the web looking for "soft" suicide measures, and even more time thumbing through books at the county library, he settled on driving his car off a cliff. Though he was afraid of heights, he figured that if he kept his eyes on the center of the steering wheel as the car approached the cliff he would not have a sensation of falling.

Mark had worked out a plan to fool his family and friends and perhaps even get a reduced sentence from God. He knew that if there were no skid marks the police would list his death as a suicide. So he planned to apply the breaks at the last minute, not soon enough to prevent the vehicle from careening over the edge, but well in advance to make it appear that he tried to stop. He was sure this would fool the police, but he wasn't so sure about God.

Two days after the 911 terrorist attacks, Mark Hipple climbed into his 1998 Ford. He buckled his seatbelt out of habit and then laughed at himself. With the deliberation of a man with his mind made up, he unbuckled the belt and smiled. He wouldn't ever need to wear the damn thing again, just like he would never have another root canal or another paper cut. Suicide had its silver lining.

He backed out of the driveway (still carefully looking for cars) and headed for an area north of the city where the highway ran along sheer cliffs, dropping several hundred feet to the rocks and ocean below. He crossed the Golden Gate Bridge, so famous for jumpers and pursued his own fate father up the California coast.

As he drove along the winding road his mind wandered. He did not question his decision to kill himself, as that was a "done deal. " But his thoughts kept turning to minutia, such as "what actually was the beef content of a McDonald's hamburger? Did politicians also lie to themselves? Why wasn't Pluto a planet anymore? Was global warming real? Why didn't Total Quality Control work in the corporate world? What if you only had a half-drop of Black blood? What was the actual cost to produce a CD? Was there a solution to the problems in the Middle East? Did the anchors on the evening news have opinions about the crap they read? Was bottled water any safer than tap water? (It was, after all, sealed in plastic). Did whores enjoy their work? Could Madonna really sing? Did Pat Garrett actually kill Wild Bill Hickok? When exactly did

Rush Limbaugh's brain turn to mush? Why did the fuck word become so popular in pop culture? Did insects pass gas like people did?

This last silly thought was ruminating around in his skull when he realized that a Fed EX truck was heading straight for him in his lane! Instinctively he swerved to avoid impact, but the truck driver must have seen what was about to happen and also turned sharply making his vehicle flip over and catch the tail end of Mark's Ford. The collision caused Mark to lose control of his car, which careened into a rock embankment.

Stunned, he looked down to see wreckage all around him. The motor was in the front seat, still churning. His seat had been broken off and he was in the back seat. He was prone on the seat and his leg hurt. He looked down to see that his femoral artery had been severed and bright red blood was vigorously being pumped onto the floorboards of the back seat. Mark had tried to become a medical doctor, then a nurse and failed at both, but he had learned enough to know that he had minutes, maybe only seconds to live if he didn't stop the bleeding. He tried to move his arms to apply pressure to his leg, but something was wrong. They wouldn't work. He watched in horror as the gush of blood got less and less, then was reduced to a trickle.

As Mark Hipple's eyes became cloudy and darkness began to press in from the edges of his vision, a delightful feeling of elation spread over him like a mother's embrace. If he hadn't been smashed up, he would have jumped for joy. As his consciousness faded to a pinpoint, he had one last thought: *God is truly merciful. I will only have to account for a life wasted on venial sins.*

30. *A New Mexico Encounter*

I'm new to New Mexico so this encounter was a bit of a shock. To say the least. One fine morning I crossed the Rio Ruidoso and climbed up into the Sacramento Mountains. First I traversed a forty-acre field, then entered the scrub brush and made my way upward, through the Piñon trees and tiny pines. It was a hot summer day and I had to stop every so often to catch my breath, as I am not used to the altitude and the heat made the climb all the more problematic for these old bones.

After several such rest stops, I made it to a small shelf or plateau in the side of the mountain. Much to my surprise I saw a wisp of smoke coming from a grove of trees situated near the base of a rocky cliff. Intrigued, I moved forward, being careful not to make any noise. I threaded myself through the trees and came within sight of what looked like a cowboy boiling coffee over an open fire.

He had on a floppy black hat, one that was not a normal Stetson-type, but more of a city-slicker hat that had been beat up pretty badly. He had on a long-sleeved grey shirt; a tan vest and he had a red bandana tied round his neck. His belt was a bandolier, that is, it had bullets in it and a six-gun hung rakishly from his hip. A pair of trousers and boots completed his outfit. His Winchester leaned against a nearby rock.

I was intrigued because he wasn't dressed like any

modern cowboy I had ever seen and, more uncharacteristically, I couldn't see a horse anywhere. While I was contemplating exactly what I should do – say hello or skirt around him – he turned and looked directly at me. "Been waitin' fer ya, Gino."

He knew my name! I must have had a fright because I took a quick step back and fell over a log right on my butt.

The cowboy guffawed a throaty sound that sounded like it came from very far away. It had a hollow sound, a sort of echo to it, like it didn't come from his camp.

"Git up off yer duff and have some coffee," said the cowboy with genuine hospitality in his voice. "Pull up a rock." He sniggered at this remark, sort of: heh, heh, heh.

I picked myself up and entered the clearing. "I was just taking a hike and saw your smoke. How did you know my name?"

He sat back on a log and smiled, showing teeth that were too big for his face. "Well, I jist sorta know stuff like that. I'm Henry – Henry McCarty. I wondered when you'd climb up here. You jist moved into the old Lone Pine ranch, didn't ya." It wasn't a question.

"Well…….well, yes. But how'd you….." That was the old name for the place, which now housed an art studio.

"Like I jist told ya, I sorta know a lot about these

here parts. Had to in the old days. Still comes in handy, it does." He pulled out a little white Bull Durham sack and began to expertly roll a cigarette. "Smoke?"

"Me? No. I gave it up years ago. Surgeon General and all that."

"Yeah, when I can I git a newspaper I read 'bout modern stuff like that, but my readin' ain't so good. I git the gist of a story but some of the new words don't register in my pea brain." Another childlike chuckle.

"Well, the government has been after people to quit smoking for health reasons."

"Yessir, I got that much, but ya see this here is one of the last little pleasures I got." He produced a kitchen match, as if by magic and quickly dragged it up his trouser leg. It burst into flame and he lit the shaggy end of his cigarette. "Help yerself," he said through a blue-grey cloud of smoke, motioning toward the coffee pot hanging over the campfire.

I moved in and poured some of the dirty brown liquid into a well-chipped enamel cup, rust showing through in several places. I was at a loss as to what I should say and blurted out: "So, where's your horse?" Once the words were out, I wished I hadn't said it. It sounded stupid.

"Oh hell, Smoke died ages ago. I seem to be all by

myself these days. You came here a couple a months ago, right?" He didn't wait for an answer and went on: "Bin inta town to see any of the sights yet?" This time he paused and took a long drag on his cigarette.

I took a sip of the coffee and quickly wished I hadn't. It had an ancient, musty taste to it. "Well, actually, no. I know that Ruidoso is a tourist town with lots of attractions though. I have been meaning to visit some of them, but you know how it is, moving in and all."

"Yessir, in my day I had to move about a fair bit too. Pick up and skedaddle. Then do it all over again. 'Bout sums up my life, it does." He sniggered again and smiled at a private joke.

There was a stiff pause in our conversation. Apparently he wasn't going to elaborate, so I asked: "You seem familiar with this territory. What would you recommend I visit first? My sisters are coming for a visit. Where should I take them?"

"Well-sir, there's the Billy the Kid Casino and the Billy the Kid Museum. Mighty popular, they are."

"Ugh, I don't think my sisters would be into going to a casino. Bit religious, they are."

"Nothin' wrong with that, fer some folks. Never got much of the Black Book larning myself." He finished his cigarette and threw it in the fire. "Take them to up to that one-horse town of Lincoln. Lots of the ole wild west there, for sure. In town here, in Ruidoso proper, you can visit Dowlin's Historic Old Mill. I used to hang around there quite a bit."

"Yes, I'm told it is still a functioning water mill."

"Dunno 'bout that. Usta be. Then outta town there's the Fort Stanton Museum, over 'n Capitan, or thereabouts. I know'd it pretty well. Actually spent some *time* near there, ya know." He smiled at another private joke. "Jist watch out for them thar Mescalero Apache. Can't trust 'em. Never could."

I found this a strange thing to say, but then the whole encounter was bizarre. I was trying to think of an exit line, when Mr. McCarty continued: "Lotta history 'round these parts, that fer sure – Lincoln County War 'n all. Was lotsa fun, that 'n."

"Yeah, wasn't that the county seat where that famous sheriff ruled the roost – Pat Garrett wasn't it?"

"Don't ya be paying him no mind. He was a gall darn liar. That he was. A gall darn devil of a liar."

Then the cowboy began to roll another cigarette and was quiet, as if far away and thinking of something private. I took advantage of the pause in the conversation to size him up. He was a short man, cocky and agile, with startling blue eyes, smooth baby-boy cheeks and very prominent teeth. He had an easygoing air about him. He chuckled to himself as he fixed his smoke. He looked up at me and his eyes twinkled, but there was something else there, deeper in his character. I thought that he could be quick tempered if provoked. I began to feel uneasy in his presence and made my apologies. "My wife will wonder where I am. Thanks for the tips about what to see hereabouts. I am sure I will find Lincoln County full of the Old West. Not much of that where I come from." I smiled, hoping to easily detach myself from his presence.

"Yeah, you New York city slickers are somethin' else again, that be fer sure."

I must have looked shocked that he knew I was from New York. As I walked away and down the hill I could still hear him laughing. There would be a time of quiet, then the haunting laugh would find its way down the mountainside. Then silence again. Half way to the house I stopped, turned and looked for the smoke of his campfire. I couldn't see any.

****

When my sisters came to visit me in New Mexico, I took them into Ruidoso to the Hubbard Museum of the American West and other "Western" attractions in town. Toward the end of the day we wound up at the hideout of Billy the Kid and then moved on to the Billy the Kid Museum. It contained a plaque that gave a short history of his life. My eyes stopped dead at one point: Billy the Kid had several aliases including Henry Antrim and William Harrison Bonney, but his real name was Henry McCarty!

31. Nigerian Nightmare

Although I knew of the Biafra War, which had taken place a decade before, the first visual indication I had of that Nigerian conflict was when I was driving north through bombed out villages, the machine gun bullet holes still visible in the mud walls of the Igbo compounds. The Igbo people had not wanted to be a part of the newly independent country of Nigeria, which they rightly saw as a colonial invention. They wanted a country of their own, which they would have called Biafra.

Then, later, when I arrived in Northern Nigeria, I saw the blood stains on the paved streets of the towns there, where largely Christian Igbo traders and shopkeepers had been dragged out in the open and slaughtered with machetes. The brilliant African sun beat down on the red-brown stains, eventually turning them white.

The Muslims of the north perpetrated this violence, while the Igbo businessmen from the southeast of the country were living in the north as traders. It was violence in the name of nationalism, or at least that was one rationalization given. The men, women and children were still dead, no matter what justifications were given.

Despite some misgivings about coming to Africa to teach, I settled in. Yet, on a daily basis, it was not a pleasant place to be. While living there, I saw much that was unpleasant. For instance, one day a man was stoned to death in the marketplace. When I inquired about the nature of his offense I was told that he was a witch, the kind that went around shaking men's hands to cause their private parts to shrivel and fall off. I thought that Sigmund Freud might enjoy the implications of this in a male-dominated, highly chauvinistic society.

"How did you know that he had this power?" I asked.

"Because someone in the market shouted that he was losing his testicles after coming into contact with this man. He shouted: Witch! Witch! And everyone nearby picked up stones and killed the evil thing."

"That *evil thing* was a human being, one who wasn't given a fair chance," I said, somewhat piously.

"Not in our way of thinking," came the reply. "If he wasn't a witch, Allah would have prevented his death."

"Oh, well that certainly explains it," I said, walking away.

At other times – too many times – I saw people hit by speeding automobiles and killed. The traffic there was horrendous. The Nigerian economy was booming in those days and everybody and his brother was buying brand new Toyotas, Audis and Mercedes cars. Many of them were chauffeured by young drivers who had never had, nor would ever get, a driver's license.   It was not uncommon to see grisly accidents on a daily basis, especially at night when one had to drive especially carefully because it was so very difficult to see black people in the darkness, which is much darker in Africa than in the Western World where roads are usually illuminated with street lights.

I also saw many head-on crashes, some rather spectacular, for instance, when two Mercedes hit each other bluntly at speeds over eighty miles per hour. In this particular fiery crash, the two vehicles became one mass of smoking, tangled metal in an instant. As it appeared that the two drivers had simply expected the other to move over, I wondered if they had ever seen the James Dean movie, *Rebel Without a Cause*. Probably not. Plain old testosterone was enough for them. They didn't need any cinemagraphic encouragement.

But, by and large, my time in Nigeria was tranquil. I lived in the native quarter, rather than in campus housing and was enjoying my time there until the *coup d'état.* My first indication that something was terribly wrong took place when, during a lecture to my sociology class, I looked out the window to see armed troops unloading from the back of a truck. Going to the window, I saw that there were many such trucks in the parking lot in front of my lecture hall. The government soldiers were moving into buildings and lecture halls, though they hadn't made it to mine at that point.

I quickly cancelled class and slipped out the back door. I don't know how I made it through campus, out the gate and to my compound in the heart of town, but I did. I sat in my garden and wondered what I had gotten myself into.

I was lucky to have African friends who hid me for over a month. The university had been shut; many of my friends had been jailed – simply for being foreigners. It soon became clear why the illegal and immoral invasion of the university had taken place. The President of Nigeria had been machine-gunned to death while driving to work. As was the norm in the nineteen seventies, the government blamed the Central Intelligence Agency. Since the CIA was "white," all whites had to go to jail as suspects.

I didn't like the logic, so I stayed home and kept my head down. I knew I could not get out of the country by driving. Every road would be blocked. It was hard enough to get in and out in normal times. Furthermore, the airports had been closed. I hunkered down.

In a little over a month the airports were opened. Friends tucked me into the trunk of my car and drove me to the Kano International Airport. We passed through several checkpoints, bribing our way through some and I finally found myself sitting in the departure lounge. Nervously.

When the call came, a line of us formed and we began to shuffle across the hot, black tarmac toward the jet that would take us away from this ugliness. I carried only a briefcase in which I had many of the articles I had recently written on African religion and a couple of others. As I looked ahead I could see that a plain clothed policeman was interrogating each person in line as he or she got to the bottom of the stairs leading up to the waiting plane.

When it was my turn he said sourly: "Open your briefcase."

I did and he reached in and pulled out the only article I had written on African politics to that point in my academic career.

"So you write about African politics?" he said with a malicious grin, which reminded me of the smirk of a cat about to eat a mouse. I was the mouse.

"Well, mostly I write about African religion," I stammered with a tongue that felt as dry as the Sahara Desert. "This article is not about Nigeria. See," I said pointing to the title, "it is about tribal politics in Ghana. Not Nigeria."

The cat looked at the mouse and smiled cruelly. The picture of the inside of a Nigerian jail flashed through my mind. It was not a pleasant image. My throat felt like someone was pouring sand down it with a funnel. The heat bouncing off the dark tarmac was excruciating. The bottoms of my feet felt like they were on fire.

The policeman pushed the paper back into my briefcase, crumbling it in the process. I didn't care. I just wanted on that plane.

He smiled unpleasantly, savoring his power. He was enjoying himself. Mouse-like, I was not having a good time. It's no fun to be dinner.

Perhaps coming to Africa has been a bad idea. All sorts of crazy thoughts and recriminations were going through my head when he nodded toward the plane, his smile having turned to a sneer. The cat wasn't hungry. In the last month, the cat had eaten mightily.

I forced myself to move slowly, trying to look calm and dignified. As I mounted the stairs I expected to hear him shout: "You there, come back!"

The people in front of me were stacked up and it seemed that the line was never going to move. I felt trapped on the white-hot steel stairs. The railing was almost too hot to touch. The African sun beat down, wicked in its delight. *This place enjoys inflicting pain. What was I thinking about in coming here? What's holding this damn line up?*

I felt like the CID man must be watching me, waiting for me to make a false move. About the only move

I had in me at this point was fainting and I surely didn't want to do that. I forced myself to think about the many good African friends I had made. I tried to use these thoughts to forget the events of the last month and the fear that was pulsating through every part of my body.

Then the line began to inch forward and I felt the fear beginning to ebb away the closer I got to the plane's cool, inviting doorway. Once I got to the top of the stairs, where I was still visible to the policeman below, one last spear-thrust of fear shot through me; and then, suddenly, I was inside and going through the familiar routine of stowing my briefcase in the overhead bin, buckling my seat belt and grabbing for a magazine.

I chanced a glance out the plane's tiny window. The secret policeman was no longer there and the intense African sun shone off the black tar of the runway, almost turning it white.

32. *The Other Side of the Street*

The sociologist had sometimes set up a little demonstration in his college classes. He would ask for volunteers from his black students and those with much whiter skins. Having selected two people with contrasting skin colors, as well as with the familiar attendant differences in hair, facial structure, etc., he would seat them facing the rest of the class and ask the students looking at them to describe the pair in a short essay.

Invariably the essays would reflect the human tendency to notice differences and ignore similarities. One was black and the other was white; but both had two legs, two arms, two ears, two eyes – you could go on forever with the *two-ness* of this train of thought. Furthermore, both had respiratory systems and the blood of each would run red in the next war the politicians thought up. Most students ignored these similarities and concentrated on the distinctions between the two. The sociology teacher had lots of ammunition for the world he considered to be so discriminatory.

The professor would then randomly select students to read their essays aloud to the group and discuss why it was that the compositions uniformly announced that one person was white and the other black; or that one had "kinky" hair, while the other did not. Cleverly, he would note all the similarities missed and lead the students into a discussion of the fact that neither was actually "white" or "black" and that "kinkyness" of hair was very difficult to define. He sometimes got bored with this exercise, its verity so evident. Some students were alert to the discussions, but others looked out the window, while yet others slumbered in the back.

Usually at this juncture an especially attentive student would point out that it was the *contrasts* people were noticing: one student was "black" in comparison to the lack of "blackness" in another.

"That's just another way of saying that one is black and the other is white – isn't it?" pointed out a brown-skinned student. The argument was on and the professor caught himself looking out the window.

The sociology teacher had been through this exercise many times over the course of a thirty-year teaching career. At times he asked the questions almost as if on autopilot. To him the subject was a truism: good people did not hate. *He* was not prejudiced and *he* was honorably engaged in putting down bigotry wherever it raised its ugly head. Often in this section of his course his mind would wander. Today the white professor's thoughts strayed to his significant other, a black woman. He could hear her shouting at her son: "Get your Nigger Ass in here!" Invariably this made his skin crawl. On other occasions she would use the N-word like polite white folk would be loath to do in public, especially in the presence of the Other.

The professor's mind was also amazed at a curious fact about which he had become aware shortly after moving in with his Island Beauty: she was prejudiced! How, he wondered, could a black woman think less of Asians, as she clearly did. "Leave it up to the Chinks," she would spit. And those "Meskins" didn't fare any better in her rantings.

Both the professor and his black partner were equally aware of police brutality in the press and were appropriately outraged when she was pulled over for a broken taillight on the truck. After all, the white professor had been driving that same vehicle for three years and not a cop thought to point out the infraction till a black person got behind the wheel. Both of them would make clucking sounds when discussing the event, which they both took as indicative of a mutual indignity and anger at the prejudice of the police.

"Waddaya 'spect?" their joint mind would say.

By way of explanation the female of the pair noted that the officer who handed her the ticket was named Chavez. "See!" she said and that was apparently enough for her to convey some deep insight to the professor. Evidently they were supposed to share some knowledge about the *Chavez-ness* of the policeman that correlated to her getting a ticket for a lousy broken taillight. "See!" they were supposed to think in unison.

To maintain their feeling of togetherness in this situation the professor held his tongue, not wanting to point out that she was *Otherizing*, as he called it in his college lectures and in his books and journal articles on injustice. After all, he had read Edward Said's influential book on what Said called *Orientalizing*. The sociologist felt a special connection to Professor Said, a noted historian, not only because he had heard Dr. Said talk once at Cambridge; but because – well – they were alike in their thinking. Wasn't *Otherizing/Orientalizing* a bad thing? Both agreed. Only bad people did such a thing and they, as authors of forward-thinking ideas, were not bad. The outraged receiver of a taillight ticket apparently did not agree. A clever man, the professor held his tongue. He did not bring up Eduard Said.

A question from a student brought the professor back from his trance-like state, from his mind-wander. He answered the question, the bell rang and the students ran for the door, clutching their cell phones to eager ears.

The professor made those same clucking sounds as he picked up his papers and stuffed them into his battered briefcase. *He* didn't own a cell phone, he proudly noted in his mind. What is the world coming to, he thought.

The room had emptied and his musing led him elsewhere as he walked across campus and through the back streets of the town to his car. He liked to think of himself as progressive and unprejudiced. It was comforting to think this way. In his introspection, as he walked into the last street before he got to the college parking lot, his mind was self-congratulatory. Though he didn't know it the professor had a smug and vainglorious look on his face as he noticed three guys in black leather jackets with brilliant frosty studs gleaming in the sun. They were walking toward him on *his* side of the street. Their garish tattoos came startlingly into view as they drew nearer. Other glistening studs projected from parts of their anatomy.

The broadminded professor made small clucking sounds as he quickly crossed to the other side of the street.

www.ingramcontent.com/pod-product-compliance
Lightning Source LLC
Chambersburg PA
CBHW030532030726
47495CB00004B/961